"Anna." Soren breathed out her name, making it a half warning but also strange and exciting. Under the heat in his eyes, she sensed a bewilderment as deep as her own and a ferocity that she found unbearably exciting.

Without breaking eye contact, he moved his fingers higher up the curve of her bare calf, then higher under the fabric as he reeled her in, pulling until her bottom was on the very edge of the sofa.

Her heart pounded out a heavy beat until she was barely breathing.

His intense magnetism seemed to be exerting a physical pull, and she found herself leaning in like he was leaning in. She recognized the moment they reached a tipping point, but not who made the final move that connected their mouths.

The heat that flared was instantaneous, the combustion seeming to consume the oxygen in the room as the slow, shatteringly sensuous exploration deepened.

Kim Lawrence lives on a farm in Anglesey with her university-lecturer husband, assorted pets who arrived as strays and never left, and sometimes one or both of her boomerang sons. When she's not writing, she loves to be outdoors gardening or walking on one of the beaches for which the island is famous—along with being the place where Prince William and Catherine made their first home!

Books by Kim Lawrence

Harlequin Presents

A Cinderella for the Desert King
A Wedding at the Italian's Demand
A Passionate Night with the Greek

Spanish Secret Heirs

The Spaniard's Surprise Love-Child
Claiming His Unknown Son

A Ring from a Billionaire

Waking Up in His Royal Bed
The Italian's Bride on Paper

Visit the Author Profile page
at Harlequin.com for more titles.

Kim Lawrence

INNOCENT IN THE SICILIAN'S PALAZZO

HARLEQUIN®
PRESENTS™

Recycling programs
for this product may
not exist in your area.

ISBN-13: 978-1-335-56948-6

Innocent in the Sicilian's Palazzo

Copyright © 2022 by Kim Lawrence

Harlequin Enterprises ULC
22 Adelaide St. West, 41st Floor
Toronto, Ontario M5H 4E3, Canada
www.Harlequin.com

Printed in U.S.A.

INNOCENT IN THE
SICILIAN'S PALAZZO

CHAPTER ONE

THERE WAS NO one at Reception. It was totally silent but for the sound of her own feet on the parquet floor.

Anna dumped her carefully packed box on the big desk that took centre stage and peered over it, careful to avoid the vase of fragrant garden roses and lavender, and stood back with a sigh of relief before she twisted the leather-bound ledger around to face her.

Pen in hand, she bent over, pinning the curtain of thick dark chestnut waves from her eyes with her forearm as she signed the visitors' book, her swirling signature a replica of many before it. You had to go back a lot of pages and many weeks to see any other signature next to the column beside her grandpa's name.

One by one his visitors had fallen away and she couldn't really blame them. Some days she approached her own visits with a sick feeling of dread in the pit of her stomach—she never knew what would await her…would he even know who she was?

Not that it would ever occur to her to not come. She owed her grandfather everything. Without him her life could have been very different—before he had stepped up to become her legal guardian, social services had been taking a lot of interest in her.

She huffed out a tiny preparatory breath before she picked up the box, her aching muscles complaining. As luck, or rather lack of it, would have it, there had been no room in the car park conveniently adjacent to the Edwardian building thanks to the shiny monster designer car that was taking up three spaces and attracting an audience of admirers.

So, courtesy of the *ridiculous* flashy car, Anna was forced to park at the main entrance the other side of the Merlin's park-like grounds, and the box that had seemed comfortably light when she had begun the trek had felt as if it weighed a ton by the time she reached the clinic.

Taking the now familiar route up to the first floor, she reached her grandfather's suite without dislodging the carefully stacked pile, and she was relieved to see the door to his private sitting room was ajar. Wedging her chin on the photo album on top and shifting the box a little higher, she turned to back cautiously into the room, bumping the door with her bottom as she did so.

'Hello, Grandpa, sorry I'm late,' she called out, wondering with a little ache of her heart if Grandpa Henry would even know who she was today. 'But wait until you see what I've got, some more photos, a lovely one of Dad and—' Tongue now caught between her teeth as she concentrated on not bumping into anything, she placed the box carefully on the bureau that had once lived in her grandpa's study at home. 'And some more of your vinyl collection—'

'You are not allowed to touch my collection. That was a very rare recording you scratched. Did you use gloves, Anna?'

'Yes, Grandpa.' The record-scratching incident had happened when she was ten.

Soren, who was standing with one hand on the headrest of the chair that held the man he had been searching for over the past twelve years, had turned at the sound of the door being opened. He had watched the entrance of the new arrival, who was totally unaware of his presence, and had seen no reason to alert her.

When Tor responded to her words, his attention shifted back to the man.

They were the first words that Tor had spoken. He caught the flicker of intelligence in the faded blue eyes for a split second before it was replaced by a cloudy belligerence.

But it had been there, and it only confirmed Soren's belief that this was an act; it *had* to be an act. He would not contemplate another option. For the past twelve years he had never lost the belief that one day he would look into the eyes of the man responsible for the destruction of his family and see fear, see the despair that must have been in his own father's eyes before he took his own life.

After years of trails growing cold and with the help of a small select team, he had finally tracked down his quarry and reached him before he pulled one of his vanishing acts. This time there would be no new identity, or new continent.

And just when you thought you had seen everything this man was capable of, that he could not get any more slippery and devious, he pulled this one out of the hat—dementia!

But when you thought about it, it made a perfect twisted sort of sense. What did a man like Tor do when he guessed the net was closing in around him and there was no place left to run? He picked out a nice place in the country with a sympathetic staff and waitress service and played his unfit-to-stand-trial card.

Soren was willing to acquit the clinic of collusion—they and the medical professionals were pawns in this latest scam. They might be unwitting accomplices but my God they had laughable security.

Soren had walked in without once being asked who he was, and his arrival had hardly been inconspicuous. Security—at least, that was what he assumed the uniformed pair had been—were more interested in his car than him.

Locating the suite of rooms occupied by Henry Randall had been straightforward too—there were names beside the numbered keys hanging on the wall. It was only when he'd entered the small sitting room that he had encountered any problem.

An unforeseen one.

Tor, ever the artiste, was deep in character.

Soren had been here ten minutes and tried everything he could think of to break through the facade. It was like coming up against a brick wall. By this point he was feeling a degree of sympathy for the professionals Tor had taken in. If Soren hadn't known what Tor was, he would have fallen for the act himself.

Totally in character, the con artist had wholly occupied the role he had chosen to play, that of a fragile, innocent, broken old man.

Struggling against the frustration banging away like a hammer against his temples, he silently berated himself for being overconfident as he dealt with a very different scenario from the one he had envisaged—which had been Tor, shocked by his unannounced appearance, betraying himself.

His initial 'Hello, Tor. It's been a while...' had drawn no response at all.

In fact Soren had seen nothing in those watery blue eyes except blankness illuminated briefly by a seemingly genuine confusion, until the disturbance in the doorway accompanied by the soft, husky voice.

Soren, whose mindset would never allow for the possibility that what he was seeing was not some sort of performance, watched with clinical interest as the figure in the upright chair raised a shaky blue-veined, waxy hand towards the figure with her back turned.

All part of the act, a *good* act, he conceded. But following this man over the years had taught Soren that it was a mistake to underestimate the cunning, twisted mind of Tor Rasmusson, who possessed the ability to run several scams simultaneously and *always* had an escape route. Over the years the man had displayed an uncanny ability to vanish like smoke, leaving carnage in his wake.

'I predict that Anna will come top in her exams...' the shrunken figure said suddenly, looking directly at Soren. 'All that girl lacks is confidence.'

The figure with her back to him, and still oblivious to Soren's presence, sighed. 'It's lovely you think I'm brilliant, Grandpa, but you're the only one.'

Soren watched as the other man glanced down at an invisible watch on his wrist.

'I have a meeting, Anna.'

Yes, with the fraud squad. Save it, Tor, Soren thought grimly as he waited for the woman to notice him.

'I hate tardiness, Anna.'

The petite figure turned and froze.

'I'm here now, Grandpa. Did you have a good night?'

The voice, pitched low and soft, held none of the wary suspicion that was now being levelled at him from a pair of eyes set in a face that on a screen just thirty-six hours ago he had casually dismissed as *almost* pretty… The below-the-belt kick that for one split second had nailed him quite literally to the spot when she had turned brought home the truth that real life, and in this case *real women*, were sometimes poorly served by pixels.

This was a *real* woman and Soren was experiencing a very real reaction to her. The flash of heat that settled in his groin was proof that his famed control had limitations.

The image had accurately recorded the proportions of her face, a face that *ought* to have been overpowered by a generous, carnally curved mouth and thick dark brows that framed wide-spaced kitten-big green eyes.

All strong features that should in theory have fought with one another, but instead they melded into a vivid, breathtakingly sensual whole.

The difference lay in part in the creamy texture of her skin, the forest green of her eyes—the lack of symmetry actually *added* to the sensual impact.

He'd have liked to see her in snug jeans, but her wide-legged linen trousers suggested legs that were proportionally long for her height, and the plaited leather belt emphasised the narrowness of her waist. The boxy baggy white shirt she wore was not meant to emphasise her sleek, slim curves but it didn't hide them.

A sound of self-disgust locked in his throat. This was not a moment to be distracted by a woman, especially if the woman in question was the granddaughter of his enemy and was probably up to her pretty neck—Soren lifted his gaze from the smooth slender column of her throat, ruthlessly leashing his hormones, before he produced a smile as he stepped forward, hand extended.

Soren had a wide repertoire of smiles; very few had anything to do with sincerity. Some instilled fear in the recipient, others melted hostility like ice cream in the sun and opened doors, frequently bedroom doors.

A faint widening of her eyes was the only indication that Anna Randall had even noticed his effort. If anything the wariness she wore like a force field seemed on the verge of tipping over into guard-dog open hostility.

Anna looked at his hand, took in the length of the long, tapering fingers.

The brief war of attrition between the deeply embedded instinct of good manners, and the shockingly shameful heat unfurling low in her pelvis that made the idea of feeling her hand in his far too attractive, ended in a draw.

Her hand stayed firmly at her side.

The faintest quirk of his lips and the hint of an ironic gleam in his eyes could have been her imagination as his hand fell away. Relieved she'd had the decision taken out of her hands, she surreptitiously rubbed her sweaty palms against her trousers and kept up the paper-thin pretence that she was immune to the stranger's cynically confident killer smile.

The muscles along Soren's angular jaw quivered, though the truth was he was more intrigued than offended by her ego-bashing attitude.

His ego was pretty robust.

There might be more to Anna Randall than her rotten gene pool and the face. He allowed his glance to skim the fascinatingly unsymmetrical, stunningly sexy features for an indulgent split second too long: the stubborn chin, the wide-spaced intelligent eyes, the smooth high cheeks, the generous carnal mouth that made him aware all over again of a hunger inside him.

Soren was not a man who avoided the truth, especially when it was staring him in the face, and the simple fact was he was attracted to the granddaughter of his enemy. The acknowledgment did not improve his mood.

'Good morning…?' She paused a split second, adding in a colder voice. 'Can I help you?'

The frigid words were polite, the suggestion underneath was anything but, but, God, she had the most *incredible* voice… Even when it was cold it had an earthy, seductive quality. Having just got his hormones in check, he didn't want to think about what it would sound like warm.

'You must be Henry's granddaughter…?' Although he allowed his voice to rise on a questioning inflection, he knew exactly who she was. The only thing about her his investigations had not revealed was just how deeply she was involved in her grandfather's latest profit-making charity fraud. That she was not involved did not even cross his mind.

Now that he had met her, he could see how useful a woman who managed to combine innocence and earthy sexiness would be to Tor. Despite the sketchy evidence, his working theory was that, as Tor's only blood relative, she was being trained to take control of the family business.

Or she might be as innocent as she appears?

He dismissed the possibility out of hand. No one related to Tor could be totally innocent. It wasn't *if* she was involved, it was how deeply.

'Yes, I'm Anna…?'

Instead of picking up on her strong verbal cue, to her frustration he ignored the silent question mark and just smiled. She fought the urge to melt and decided that he rarely had to do anything beyond smile to sidestep any question.

'I had imagined you being older,' he responded truthfully, and saw the questioning flicker in her eyes again, though actually he *had* imagined her looking older. He knew her age was… The exact number had not stayed with him, but she barely looked twenty, let alone mid-twenties. 'I understand that you have inherited… Henry's love of books? Librarian, that must be interesting…?'

She didn't react to the question but she had

dialled down her antagonism a notch or two;
he was making the effort but Soren still wasn't
feeling the love.

'Are you another journalist?'

Nothing in his face showed he had noted the
another. 'Do I look like a journalist?'

'What do journalists look like?' Few, she conceded, could have worn the sort of exclusive-
looking suit he was wearing. 'So if you're *not*,
just who are you exactly?' Beyond quite obviously the most sinfully good-looking man she
had ever seen or even dreamt existed.

It had initially taken her a couple of startled
blinks to take in the superficial details, namely
his height, several inches over six feet, the immaculate tailoring, steel-grey suit and a tie a few
shades paler lying against a snowy white shirt,
which gave an air of steely exclusivity and did
not disguise the fact his broad-shouldered frame
was lean and athletically powerful.

Now she was taking in details beyond the
way his hair hugged his shapely skull but was
long enough to curl against his collar and was
worn swept back casually from a broad brow. It
framed symmetrical features that were set in a
square-jawed face that was all hollows and angles, slanted cheekbones sharp enough to cut, an
aquiline nose and a carved mouth that required
a blink in its own right, a firm lower lip and a

full, overtly sensual upper. But it was his eyes that were the real showstopper—bluer than any blue she had ever seen, not warm sky blue but arctic-ice blue, and were set beneath the dark ebony bars of his brows and framed by crazily long sooty dark lashes.

Now she was taking in the intelligence in the eyes, the ruthlessness suggested by the firm lower lip and his armour-plated aura of raw masculinity.

Not that this set her apart from any other woman with a heartbeat; this was a man who no doubt took female admiration as a given.

Annoyed that she was fulfilling his smug expectations, and determined not to give him the satisfaction of knowing her stomach was quivering violently, she kept her expression still and filed this disturbing fact away for later consideration, swallowing a couple of times to lubricate her dry throat and ignoring how her legs still felt disconnected from her body.

Luckily they carried her without incident to her grandfather's side. She smiled down as the claw-like hand caught her own before he reached out awkwardly for the glass of water just out of reach.

'So how do you know my grandfather, Mr...?'

'Sorry, I thought I had said,' he lied smoothly.

'Soren, Soren Vitale, your grandfather was my late father's…*mentor* way back when.'

Aware in the periphery of her vision of the hand extended once more towards her, Anna listened to the inner voice that told her it would be a bad idea to feel those long brown fingers close over her own…mainly because the idea was so attractive.

Eye contact had just about shredded her nervous system so skin contact was definitely something to avoid, she decided as she carefully pushed the glass towards her grandfather, dragging out the process until hiding behind her hair was no longer an option without looking a little deranged.

She lifted her head, experienced the grab of those blue eyes, the jolt finally reaching her toes, and she could breathe.

'I'm sorry…'

'It was a long time ago.'

'Mentor?' Unable to ignore the hand any longer, she allowed her fingers to touch his. By this point she would have been surprised if there *hadn't* been the tingle of an electric shock, she decided as she surreptitiously rubbed her hand against her thigh.

'When your grandfather had…' He paused and the blue focus shifted a little to her left. Free of the full beam, she compressed her lips against a sigh of relief. 'When he had business interests in Iceland. They shared offices outside Reykjavik.'

'Iceland...?' She shook her head, the absurd suggestion tugging her lips into a condescending smile. 'I think you're mistaken. You *are* mistaken. My grandfather has never been to Iceland,' she told him firmly.

The dark brows lifted as his hooded eyes watched her. 'He never spoke of his time there?'

His intense scrutiny made her shift uncomfortably. 'I think,' she began crossly, 'I would have known if my grandfather...' She paused, remembering the long unexplained absences, though in truth it was the gifts that always accompanied his return that had stuck in her mind as a child. 'I suppose it's possible...' she conceded reluctantly.

'What reason would I have to lie about such a thing?'

Anna shrugged but didn't acknowledge he had a point.

'How about we go back to the moment you walked in? I can supply character references if you like?'

His sarcasm and the gentle mocking smile that played across his carved lips made her skin heat. 'I was surprised. I didn't know my grandfather had visitors. There were no names in the book when I signed in.'

An unconvincing look of dismay spread across his face and his smile came with attractive crinkles that fanned out from his spectacular eyes, eyes that held no humour or warmth, just a soul-dissecting intensity.

'Oh, dear, have I broken the rules?'

Oh, yeah, and you're really going to lose sleep over that, aren't you? she thought, allowing her gaze to travel upwards from his feet to the top of his attractively ruffled dark head.

'They are quite strict here at the Merlin,' she retorted primly. 'People staying here are very vulnerable.'

Soren watched as she planted a protective hand on the back of her grandfather's chair and thought, *Sure, vulnerable like a wolf.*

'And yet your journalist slipped in…?'

Unable to contradict this observation—she had sent an email to the management that said as much—she kept her lips clamped tight.

'Odd name that for a…place.' He looked around the room that, despite the half-panelled walls and the antique furniture, still held the clinical paraphernalia of a hospital, including a mobile oxygen tank. He had to admit the window dressing was convincing.

'Place?'

His mobile eyebrows twitched into a straight line above his hawkish nose. 'Like this.'

'Merlin was the original owner's stage name. Back in the Edwardian era he was a magician, quite famous, he owned several hundred acres, although now there is just the house and gardens.' She had reached the point where she knew she sounded like a guidebook when she felt her grandfather's hand go limp in her own.

She glanced down and saw that he had fallen asleep, his head to one side.

Her throat ached with emotion and sadness as she pulled her hand free. He looked so vulnerable it was hard to imagine he had until recently been a person with the sort of presence that could fill an auditorium—she had seen it happen and been proud when the people sitting there had been inspired by one of his lectures. She lifted a hand to her mouth to hide the quiver she had no control over.

'So how long has he been here?'

Her head lifted and she found he was watching her with a disturbing intensity. 'Six months. Sorry if I sounded, as if… The staff caught a journalist in here last week.' Her anger sparked green flame in her eyes at the memory. 'People are… He'd hate anyone to see him like this and, actually, no one does,' she said, unable to keep the bitterness from creeping into her voice.

'Your grandfather is not allowed visitors?'

'He's allowed but…he had visitors before his condition deteriorated…'

He watched as she lifted a hand and, under the cover of brushing strands of hair from her brow, took the moments it required to steady her voice, which was flat and expressionless as she delivered the bleak addition.

'He doesn't recognise people nowadays.'

If this was an act on her part, it was good, Soren admitted, watching the muscles in her slender throat contract as she blinked to clear her tear-misted eyes and lifted her chin, unwilling to own the emotional vulnerability she was vibrating.

Soren weighed the possibilities. It *could* be that she was not privy to her grandfather's act…? That would, he mused, watching as the emotions she was struggling to suppress played across the surface of her face, explain her seemingly genuine reaction.

It would require an utterly heartless bastard to put his only blood relative through that sort of hell, but that was not an issue for a man like Tor.

'I imagine that dementia scares people, embarrasses them…maybe it makes them conscious of how fragile life is?' Soren knew all about the fragility of life.

He stood, head tilted a little to one side, his stance relaxed as, with hands thrust deep into the pockets of his tailored trousers, he watched his words flash shocked recognition in her eyes before she slowly nodded.

Her wariness remained but she no longer looked likely to clobber him with the nearest blunt object as she turned her gaze to the chair and its occupant.

There was a gentle snore and Tor had slumped lower in the armchair… It was a sight that would have wrenched the hardest of hearts, but Soren had no doubt that this was part of the act—the authenticity helped by a physical frailness. But then everyone got older.

Including him. He doubted he bore any resemblance to the seventeen-year-old who had walked into the barn that day and seen… He had no idea how long he had stood guard over his father's lifeless body before a neighbour had found him.

'It does scare them… People who last year worked closely with my grandfather…' Something about his presence and his vague explanation for it still seemed not right to her.

The silence lasted for several heartbeats, as did the unblinking regard of those ice-chip-blue eyes. Anna wanted to look away but couldn't have if her life had depended on it; the mesmerising stare had grabbed her in a vicelike grip.

'Iceland is small, population wise, everyone knows one another and for some time your grandfather was almost like one of the family.'

They had invited the enemy into their home. There had been warm cosy family dinners. Tor had been sympathetic to Soren's teenage problems, listening when he moaned about his parents. He had always seemed interested and genuine, Soren remembered, making unfavourable comparisons with his own father.

It turned out that Tor's only interest had been in emptying his father's company's pension fund.

It's all gone, Soren, there's nothing left.

His father's words, the sound of utter bleakness, had stayed with him. They would never leave him; they were branded into his memory along with the images.

His mesmeric blue stare had moved away and she felt her shoulders sag, could breathe again. 'Vitale? I don't actually recall…'

'Not Vitale… Steinsson.' The ice-flecked blue eyes were back on full soul-stripping beam as they landed on her face. 'When I moved to Sicily after my father's death, I added my mother's family name.' Not out of choice—it was part of the deal that made his mother's future safe.

Biagio Vitale did not give anything for nothing, and Soren had not been in a strong negotiating position.

Feeling like a bug under a microscope, Anna

shook her head. 'Sorry, he might have…' Her brow wrinkled. 'Vitale sounds a little familiar,' she conceded.

Probably because she had to have at least one gleaming luxury kitchen appliance that carried the logo. Most people did. Though of course the arms of the Vitale empire were not all so visible to the general public, except in their individual fields. The engineering arm, the financial services, both had a global reputation, but the jewel in the multibillion-pound crown was claimed by the green initiatives that had been Soren's first act as CEO. His diversion of funds from oil and gas exploration was no longer considered an insane gamble.

'It was a long time ago.'

To the rest of the world it was old news. Not for Soren. He had lived the story: the disgraced businessman took his own life after he was caught stealing the pension fund of his employees.

Except he hadn't, his only crime had been trusting his friend and partner, Tor Rasmusson, who had vanished along with the money leaving a trail of financial breadcrumbs that led to Stein Steinsson.

The loss of her husband and the scandal had been too much for his mother, Hanna, who had spiralled into a deep depression then total breakdown.

Seventeen, angry and helpless, Soren had stopped being the straight-A student overnight. He'd got into fights defending his father even though he had been angry as hell with him for leaving them. He had made a point of mixing with the wrong crowd.

Maybe he would have fulfilled the many predictions that he would go off the rails and end up in jail as popular opinion said his father should have, if he hadn't found the stash of tablets his mother was hoarding and the letter she had written ready for the day she would use them.

It had been his wake-up call. He knew then that he needed help, not the sort of help being offered. He didn't need a counsellor, or therapist; he needed a safe place for his mother.

His options were limited.

There was no one, just him, so he swallowed his pride and approached his Sicilian grandfather, the man who had cast off his only daughter when she had ignored the dynastic merger of an arranged marriage and run away with her long-haired Icelandic lover, her Viking, who at the time had been hitchhiking around Europe.

Biagio Vitale was not about to be swayed by a sob story—he did not do sentiment, he did business—and he agreed to offer his daughter a sanctuary and the best professional help money could buy, but in return he wanted Soren body and soul.

He had no heir, and if after eight years Soren had proved himself he would have the option of running the Vitale conglomerate, but in those eight years he would go where Biagio sent him and do as he was told—learn from the bottom up and expect no favours for who he was.

There were no favours but there was a lot of hostility for the rich boy who wanted to be their boss from the hard men who made their living working in hot, sweaty and often dangerous conditions in the oil rigs and steel mills, and from managers who had worked hard to get to the middle, testing the hell out of this kid who had a free ride to the top. Except it wasn't a free ride. In the end he won respect and even made some unlikely friends.

At the end of eight years Soren was in a position to set his own conditions and he never forgot the reason he was where he was.

He knew the truth and one day so would the world. He would clear his father's name.

CHAPTER TWO

'WELL, IT WAS very thoughtful of you to come. I just wish that Grandpa Henry—'

Soren watched as her sad, shadowed green eyes slid to her grandfather's face. Whatever the truth, her emotion seemed genuine.

'I know he would have appreciated it,' she said, struggling to feel any personal gratitude for his effort.

There was just *something* about this man... aside from the very obvious that made Anna *uneasy*, beyond the discovery that she had a weakness for a pretty face, or in his case *beautiful*. She made the private concession with reluctance mingled with exasperation as her gaze was drawn back to his mouth, a mouth that invited fantasies.

Horrified by the one that sprang fully formed into her head involving the silken touch of his tongue, the slick, warm... She gave a panicky little gasp, pressed a protective hand to her stomach and picked up one of the framed photos. She stared at it blindly for a few sense-calming moments before she made herself look at him with a painted smile that felt in imminent danger of cracking as shock and shame continued to ricochet through her.

She pretended that the biggest problem in her world was the angle of the photos on the shelf and cleared her throat before asking brightly, 'I hope you haven't come too far out of your way?'

To her relief and surprise she sounded sane and not at all like someone who had mentally undressed him the moment she laid eyes on him.

'Not at all.'

Anna pretended not to notice the edge of mockery underlying his response—anything she said was only going to prolong this conversation.

'About the security. You might like to suggest they beef it up.'

Her lips tightened. Did he imagine she hadn't already? Repressing an acid retort, she tipped her head in acknowledgment.

'So what was this journalist after?'

My God, was he ever going to go?

Slowly she turned around to face him. 'I have no idea, but look at Grandpa Henry—what sort of person…?' She clamped her lips, squeezing them to a bloodless white as she fought to contain the surge of anger that made her chest heave dramatically against the loose white cotton that Soren discovered was semi-transparent. 'What motivates someone like that?'

Soren arched one of the dark thick brows that framed his startling blue eyes. 'Who knows?' he said lightly. He was not interested in motivation or rehabilitation, he wanted revenge.

'*Anyone* with a conscience,' she snapped and then felt guilty because he hadn't done anything except make her…she began to think about the heat that had…and stopped the thought in its tracks before it reached critical mass.

'A mistake to assume that everyone has one,' Soren said, looking at the figure in the chair. 'You'd be surprised how many don't.'

A lack of conscience would ironically have won his own grandfather's approval a lot sooner; a good deal of his training had involved eradicating this undesirable trait.

'So, goodbye, then, Mr—'

'Soren.'

'Goodbye,' she said firmly. 'I don't want to be rude…but I think you should go.'

For a brief unguarded moment astonishment washed over his face; a second later his sense of irony kicked in at this role reversal.

Taste of your own medicine, Soren!

Though in his own defence he was generally less blunt when he walked away from a woman.

Anna missed the brief interplay of emotions that slipped through his guard. She had begun to remove the items she had packed into the box, more photos to join those already on the wall and shelves. The music her grandfather loved, a couple of leather-bound volumes of his favourite novels... Anything that was familiar made him feel more secure.

Unaware of the wistful smile that tugged at her lips, she straightened a framed photo of her parents, the dad she didn't remember and the beautiful mother who was...well, who knew where?

Anna's smile deepened as she thought of her absent parent—beautiful, selfish, but she never pretended to be anything else and Anna had stopped being angry with her unmaternal mother a long time ago. She was no longer the little girl dumped quite literally on some often resentful friend's doorstep because her mum felt the urge to trek in the Amazon or spend some quality time cleansing her chakras in a Himalayan retreat.

Soren stared at the set of her slender back. He found himself struggling to appreciate the novelty value of being ignored and virtually dismissed by a woman, and, even though he had been about to leave, found himself lingering.

Could she really be what she appeared, which was a concerned, loving granddaughter oblivious to her grandparent's sordid history?

Normally he could rely on his instincts but he found himself resisting them. He was wired to mistrust any blood relation of Tor, but it was more complicated than that. He was strongly sexually drawn to her—were hormones clouding his judgment?

Was her mouth clouding his judgment?

He resented the idea; he resented questioning his own judgment.

For some reason he found himself wanting to make her look at him again. 'So when I come again I will sign in.'

Anna's quiet smile said she knew he wouldn't come again.

'Who are you?'

At the aggressive growl the photo she was holding slipped to the floor. Not that she appeared to register the sound of breaking glass. Soren watched as she closed her eyes, braced her slender shoulders and painted on a smile before turning around to face the hostile suspicion being directed at her by a now fully awake Tor.

'Hello, Grandpa, it's Anna. I came to visit. I brought you some things, some photos from your study and—'

'Who are you?'

'The book we were reading…would you like—?'

There was the vicious expression in Tor's watery pale eyes and he tried to rise from his chair but collapsed weakly back. 'Help, thief…put that down!'

She tensed, her soothing calm paper thin, and she pitched her voice to a coaxing gentle murmur. 'It's me, Grandpa… A-Anna.'

Despite all her effort her voice cracked emotionally. She knew it was the disease not her grandpa speaking, throwing out the wild insults, but it was always heartbreaking to witness.

His mood could change without warning; the episodes of aggression that turned him into a stranger were occurring with more and more frequency.

She flashed Soren a look tinged with desperation. 'Please go,' she said, reacting instantly to her deeply embedded protective instincts, moving to shield her grandfather from this uninvited guest's scrutiny. Heartbreaking enough that this disease had robbed Grandpa Henry of his dignity without there being an audience.

Soren didn't say anything; he had no intention of going anywhere.

'I know what they think but I didn't kill anyone!'

'Grandpa, no one is saying that.' She gasped, horrified at the idea he was lost in this nightmare.

'It wasn't me…he was weak and stupid. What sort of man deserts his family?' he spat out contemptuously.

Every muscle in Soren's body clenched. It was only by a cosmic effort of will that he didn't challenge the man sitting there taunting him. The insidious pity that had been creeping up on him instantly died, because this performance was for him, of that there could be no doubt.

'Who are you?' He turned to Soren. 'Get her out of here, Stein. I have a very important meeting… Where is everyone?' As abruptly as it had emerged the aggression seemed to drain out of him, leaving a tired, shrunken old man sitting there.

'I'm here,' Anna soothed.

'Get her away from me!'

'Please don't be afraid. I'm…' She saw his face change once more, saw the anger, but as always it was the fear she could sense underneath, worse even than the fact that the angry words that fell from his lips had no meaning, that he didn't recognise her—he was *afraid* of her—that cut the deepest.

Blinking back tears, she told herself fiercely that this *wasn't* him, not Grandpa Henry, as she began to slowly back away.

It broke her heart; he was in there some-where, lost.

'I'm going, it's fine, I'll get Tanya or Will… or—' Her progress came to an abrupt halt as she backed into solid male.

The impulse to lean into the warm, solid strength was hard to resist, but she was used to standing on her own feet.

A rock face would have had more give. Before she could compose herself enough to pull away, hands came to rest lightly on her shoulders. They were large and heavy, not restraining her. She stood there for a moment breathing in the scent of his soap, feeling the warmth of his body, the strength of this stranger's hands.

She was seized by an irrational conviction that if she could absorb some of his strength, she could cope with the fact her grandfather was waving his walking stick at her and yelling what was probably meant to be abuse but was unin-telligible.

If hearts really did break hers would be lying on the floor right now in a million pieces.

She was willing back the tears she knew were shining in her eyes as she attempted to pull away. For a moment he didn't react to her murmured *sorry* and a request for him to get a nurse.

When the pressure of his big hands lifted she felt strangely ambivalent about the broken physical contact, which was ridiculous. She had been standing on her own feet for… Well, for ever, really. There had only ever been Grandpa Henry standing between her and being totally alone, and now there was…no one. Straightening her shoulders and tugging herself free of this spiral into pathetic self-pity, she went to move forward but the visitor, still ignoring her request to fetch help, stepped past her.

Soren swore softly under his breath, it went against his every instinct to play the old man's game, but watching her radiate hurt as she fell totally for Tor's act had nudged his dormant protective instincts into inconvenient life. One thing the scene had revealed was that there could be no doubt at this point that for his granddaughter this pretence was real.

While it didn't mean she didn't know, and that she might be deeply involved in the illegal house of cards that was about to crash down on her grandfather was still a question mark, she did believe Tor's act and no one deserved that.

Anna was so distracted by the tactile quality of the authoritative delivery that she didn't even register they were not words, just sounds, not until her grandfather, a smile now lighting his face, repeated them.

'Hun ein vinur…?'

The way her grandfather repeated the gibberish carefully, his eyes seeking reassurance from the tall stranger who stood with his back to her, broke her heart all over again. Instead of acknowledging the hurt, she embraced her anger, fanning the flame into hot life as she stepped forward and grabbed the mocking stranger's arm, registering as she did so the hard tensile strength of the muscles.

She was ashamed of the flip low in her belly, her self-disgust lending her extra strength as she grabbed the fabric and yanked hard, making him react.

As he turned to face her she angled her furious glare upwards—a *long way* upwards. The shock of contact with the sheer cold, calculating fury living in the blue depths of his deep-set eyes made her mind blank.

Then it was gone, like a mirage or a trick of the light.

'Don't make fun of him!' she managed to snap out before her breath snagged hard on the emotional rock in her chest, making further comment impossible. She just hated it when she got so mad she wanted to cry.

'I was not *making fun*.' It was no less a ludicrous interpretation, as anyone who knew him would have told her, than *I was being kind*.

She felt the thread of anger inside her unravelling. The eyes looking back at her were the bluest thing she had ever seen in her life, the piercing quality emphasised by dark iris rings and the framing of ebony eyelashes that were impossibly long and sooty black against the equally startling backdrop of a face that was all strong, perfect angles.

A face dissected by a strong nose, high razor-edged cheekbones, a square chin with the suggestion of a cleft and a mouth that was both sensual and cruel.

It was her reaction to his mouth that made her rush into speech, almost falling over her words in her haste to not think about the shameful pulse of heat between her legs.

'I want you to leave, now!'

'Stein!'

Everything inside Soren froze for the second time as he spun around in time to see the warm charming smile he remembered from his youth.

Before he could react the smile was gone and there were tears rolling down Tor's lined cheeks.

In the periphery of his vision Soren was conscious of the small stricken figure who stood there clenched with misery as she witnessed a performance that was clearly directed at him. But then Tor never had cared about inflicting collateral damage.

Even had he fallen for it, Tor's effort was wasted. There was zero chance of pity work-

ing its way through Soren's defences. Even if
he could rid himself of the conviction that behind the fragility of the shaking hands and the
milky pale incomprehension in the pale blue
eyes the old man was secretly laughing at him,
Soren would *never* have been able to feel pity.
That would have been the ultimate betrayal of
his father.

'It's me, Grandpa…it's Anna.'

Pitched to a soothing low murmur, the sup-
pressed pain in each shaky syllable held stark,
raw grief.

Looking at her, Soren felt some nameless thing
break loose in his chest. She looked bone-ach-
ingly tired, numb with exhaustion. He could see
the quiver of fine muscles under the smooth pallor of her impossibly clear skin—like a road map
of her emotions close enough to the surface for
him to feel.

He wanted to unhear the pain; it awoke memories of his mother's hurt. Hurt that he had
soothed as best his seventeen-year-old self could
and she, oblivious to the fact he didn't have a
clue how he was going to fulfil his promise of
making things right, or what taking responsibility for another person actually entailed, had
seemed to take comfort from his words—she'd
believed him.

He had never articulated it, not even to himself, but the knowledge that he would never voluntarily take responsibility for another human being again had become part of him during the following months. It had become his emotional fingerprint.

He wasn't going to offer to make this woman feel better, and, if he had, he was pretty sure she would have thrown any offer of comfort back in his face, along with any blunt object that came to hand, he decided, studying her face, not an unpleasurable pastime. This was not a scared woman seeking reassurance.

This was a woman regaining ground she had lost and setting boundaries.

Boundaries that placed him the other side of a very high wall. It was a novel sensation for Soren, who was accustomed to people placating and ingratiating themselves with him.

Her eyes were cool green ice now on his face, which was good because he needed to cool down.

'You've done your duty, and for that thank you, but talking gibberish back to my grandfather is not helpful it…is…*demeaning*…' Her voice shook with anger that still held her rigid. 'He's not a…my grandpa Henry is still in there somewhere!'

I could tell you some things about your grandpa

Henry, he thought, watching as she moved as if to body-block her grandfather from him.

So why aren't you telling her, Soren?

She was going to know soon. The world was about to know it all, he had made sure of that.

'The words make sense in his head,' she explained. 'They just—'

Soren hesitated. The internal battle was brief. It was deeply frustrating to realise that despite his grandfather's years of training he had retained more scruples than he would own to.

'They do make sense.'

'To him, yes, but—'

He ignored her, dismissing her interruption. 'He is speaking Icelandic.'

'My grandfather doesn't speak—' She paused and bit her lip as her grandfather began to speak over her.

Soren was good at multitasking. He could listen to Tor predicting the Icelandic banking meltdown of decades earlier and watch as his protective granddaughter chucked Soren a rot-in-hell look.

The irony was, of course, she was too late to protect her grandfather, at least from the truth, which Soren had already selectively leaked to cause maximum impact... He ignored the scratch of guilt and told himself that that old man didn't deserve such dedication and, while he was willing to admit that his granddaughter seemed genuinely ignorant of his previous life, she seemed more than capable of looking after herself and there were others out there who deserved the truth, others who had lost everything because of Tor.

Anna's teeth clenched as the stranger ignored her and responded to her grandfather, speaking fluent gibberish back.

'I asked you not to—' She stopped as she watched her grandfather's face light up. Eagerness she had forgotten about lit his eyes as he responded with a convincing fluency that was not necessarily significant given her grandfather's confusion.

He didn't seem confused now, he sounded more animated than he had in weeks, and now that she listened she heard a pattern, a repetition in the words that she had never noticed before— because she had not been listening for them.

She was dealing with the first quiver of nagging doubt when she registered that her grandfather was looking at her, his white brows raised in enquiry.

'He is asking if you have done your homework,' Soren translated, recognising that the chances were Tor was never going to drop the act.

If it was an act?

He pushed the thought away. 'Maths homework.'

'It's true?' She searched his face. 'You *understand* what he's saying?'

'I do.'

'So all the time we thought he was... Tell him—' Before she could ask the stranger to translate for her the walking stick fell from her grandfather's limp clasp and his eyes closed.

'He's asleep...?'

Soren turned his head from the figure in the chair in time to see her nod in response. Her luminous eyes were fixed on the old man, an entire world of emotion chasing across her expressive features. In the unguarded moment, her face had a piercing vulnerability.

He looked away, feeling he'd intruded on something intensely private.

'He can't sleep at night, it's part of his condition. When he was at home,' she continued, her expression abstracted, her voice so soft now it was almost as if she was talking to herself rather than him, 'I had to lock the doors. The police found him wandering in the park in his pyjamas.'

'You cared for him at home?' He could only imagine what that would entail, but he was sure it would have included putting her own life on hold. He had some experience of having a grandparent take over your life, but his had been a bargain with benefits—it seemed hard to imagine any benefits for this woman.

'For a while.'

'So you were essentially his carer?'

'For a short time.' At least he didn't seem about to acclaim her *selfless* actions, Anna thought, which was a relief. His faint disapproval was preferable to being viewed as either a saint or an object of pity.

'No sleep at night but in the day…he just drops off without warning in the middle of drinking a cup of tea sometimes. He had a bad night and—'

She broke off, her eyes lifting from the slumped sleeping figure to the man standing by the door, his broad shoulders propped against the wall, his eyes fixed on her face. The piercing blue regard made her shift uncomfortably and she bent to pick up the broken glass, wincing as a bubble of blood appeared on her fingertip.

He was pleased to hear her swear crudely. A moment later she flashed him a rueful look and pulled her finger from her mouth and, aware of the sleeping figure, whispered, 'Sorry,' as she rose to her feet, sucking her finger, which immediately drew his attention to her lips with uncomfortable results.

'I've heard worse.'

It was the first genuine grin she'd seen… Oh, my God, he really was sinfully beautiful! She dropped her head and made a meal of extracting a tissue from her pocket. By the time she'd wrapped it around her oozing finger her blush had reduced by a few shades.

'I need to clear up the—'

'Leave that for someone else to clear,' he snapped out in exasperation. 'You should get that attended to.' He caught her hand. 'Let me see,' he said, not looking at her finger but at her face...and Anna was looking back.

She had no idea how long the frozen-in-time heart-racing moment lasted, and it was Soren who broke it, letting her hand fall without a word.

'Heavens, it's just a scratch,' she said. 'I'm fine.' Well, she would be once her heart slowed to near normal. 'I don't understand any of this—is it really possible? All the time we thought... he was confused.'

Confused like the evil old fox he was, or even if he was genuinely ill, either way Soren could think of several million reasons why Tor Rasmusson did not deserve her sympathy or her dedication.

'Oh, poor Grandpa!'

Poor Grandpa! It took all his self-control for Soren not to inform this woman just what her *poor* grandpa was capable of, the muscles along his jaw quivering and his nostrils flaring in disgust as his narrowed gaze took in the pathetic figure in the chair.

Anna swallowed and lifted a hand to her head. 'You made him laugh. I haven't heard him laugh for a long time. How can he speak Icelandic? This is all so…' She lowered her voice. 'Can we talk…outside?' She glanced from the sleeping figure to the open door.

Soren followed her towards the door, happy to comply; he hated to be breathing the same air as that man.

Anna's head was spinning. She had no idea how her grandfather spoke the language of a country that up until today she had never known he had even visited. Perhaps, she speculated, it was a long time in the past, like the old music the staff played that soothed him. He still remembered things long gone with amazing clarity sometimes; it was the present that he struggled with.

Anna walked a few feet down the corridor to where a few easy chairs were set into a square bay window that looked out onto a small landscaped quadrangle.

She didn't sit down but turned towards him. 'Thank you for that.'

'For what?'

'That is the most like himself I've seen him in a long time… I know he speaks French and

a little German but *Icelandic*! It never crossed
my mind or anyone else that he was actually—
I suppose I'd better get a phrase book.' She
began dragging a hand through her hair where
the natural titian highlights in the deep dark
brown caught the sun shining in through the
window. 'I know it's a lot to ask but if you're
ever nearby…?'

He saw where she was going with this and
spared her further embarrassment by cutting in
coolly. 'I do not live in this country.'

He watched as she struggled to hide her disappointment; she managed a rueful smile. 'Of
course. But now that I know…and that is down
to you.' Her smile hit his underused conscience
yet again.

Recalling her snarling initial reaction, Anna
wasn't surprised by his lack of response to her
heartfelt apology. He looked like a man who
was in a hurry to escape and who could blame
him? She felt that way sometimes. He had come
to pay his respects to an old friend of his father, not to be accused of some sort of nameless crime.

She gave an embarrassed grimace; she had
wanted him to leave and now she felt a strange
reluctance to see him go. 'I was so rude to you.
I'm sorry…'

Soren marvelled at how easily she said the

words that he struggled with, that his own grandfather had taught him to associate with weakness and failure. Personally he had always found the words empty, but when Anna Randall used them she seemed to mean it.

'I do not melt at harsh words.'

As he pushed away the apology with a flick of his long fingers, the gesture and his deep voice suggestive of impatience, she picked up his faint accent for the first time.

'I still don't understand!' she said, confusion showing in her green eyes. 'I know Grandpa had interests abroad with the charity—he was very hands-on and totally committed.'

For a moment the temptation was there to disillusion her, tell her that the man, the *saint* figure, she was grieving for never existed.

The moment passed, not because he rose above his instincts, but because he knew that she would learn the truth soon enough.

For the moment her ignorance was bliss, if it was true. She had no inkling she would soon be at the centre of a media feeding frenzy when the story broke.

And who knew? Maybe she wasn't the innocent she appeared. Aware that his *wanting* her to be complicit in her grandfather's crime, even though it was patently obvious she thought her grandparent was some sort of saint, was in part an effort to ease his own guilt brought a self-contemptuous sneer to his lips.

Maybe it was time she woke up to the truth. He hesitated. It might be time for her to wake up to the truth, but he found he didn't much want to be the one personally doing the waking.

'Iceland? So you are Icelandic...?' She had heard it was called the land of ice and fire and the description could have fitted this man with his ice-blue eyes that could flare with flame. It was really not a stretch to see him as some sort of sexy Viking.

'On my father's side. I heard from a mutual acquaintance of this situation, and—'

'He remembers you? He called you Stein...?'

'My father, though we are not alike—he died very young.' He paused, shielding his expression as the image that had haunted him down the years floated into his head.

'How many other secrets does he have?' she wondered out loud before raising her gaze to this man who might have some of the answers to the hundred questions in her head. 'Do you still live—?'

'We moved away some years ago,' Soren cut in smoothly. 'My mother is Sicilian by birth.'

Sicilian, well, that explained his vibrant colouring. His ice-blue eyes were the only evidence of his northern genes.

'I still don't understand any of this. My grandfather never mentioned—'

'It is hard sometimes to think that our parents, and I suppose that goes doubly for grandparents, had a life before we came along—like us, they have their own secrets.'

It was only the knowledge that it would make her sound boring that stopped her blurting that she had no secrets.

'I suppose you're right... I wish I knew though.'

Be careful of what you wish for, he thought, feeling an unexpected and unwelcome stab of sadness for her soon-to-be-lost innocence.

She looked up, smiling. 'I wish you'd known him...before...seeing him yelling that way...he never raised his voice to me. He was such a decent and honourable man, everyone loved him.'

A nerve jumped in Soren's lean cheek. Not everyone, and soon maybe no one, but he knew without doubt that she would cling to her illusions for as long as she could.

And when they were gone? He left the thought unfinished. That was not his responsibility. There were a lot of people out there, a lot of victims who deserved the truth.

'He was...' Her eyes moved past him. 'It's Dr Greyson.' A smile on her face, she moved past him to meet the group who were walking towards them.

Soren could hear several staff members greeting Anna by name as he turned in the opposite direction and walked away.

CHAPTER THREE

SOREN LIFTED A hand to his jaw and felt the rough growth of stubble. He had arrived at the London office of the Vitale Group the previous evening direct from the Merlin clinic, drawing a look of reproach from his superbly organised PA, Natalie, who had arrived the day before. She had already sorted every detail of the complex meetings scheduled for the following day... which was, Soren realised as he glanced out of the panoramic plate-glass windows that revealed the wide-awake city below, today.

'You're a distraction.'

'Where's the respect? The—?'

'Obsequious boot-licking...? Wrong PA. Also, I worked for you before you were infallible and a financial genius.'

Soren had grinned and retreated to his office because that was where he'd been heading anyway. He glanced down now, his lip curled in mild distaste as he took in his creased suit. He would definitely be a distraction if he rolled up looking like this, or start rumours of all-night partying.

He grabbed the jacket hooked over the back of his chair, and shook it out. He hadn't been partying, he'd worked through the night, which was not unusual—he liked the lack of distractions his days were filled with.

Except last night there had been distractions, mostly in his own head. Tor had robbed him of the moment he had dreamt of all these years.

Not that he was escaping justice—sure, his diagnosis, faked or real, might make him personally untouchable, but Tor's sins had caught up with him and very soon his reputation would be trashed along with the reputations of all those who had conspired with him.

It felt like coming second in a race, and Soren had never seen the point in that, and being forced to accept it now did not sit well with him.

Unbidden, the face of Anna Randall floated into his head. The green eyes seemed to look at him reproachfully. He swore, she really was too good to be true…but if, as he suspected, she was… He rose in one restless fluid motion, and, jacket slung across his shoulder, dragged a hand through his already ruffled hair.

If she was about to have her eyes opened, she ought, he told himself sourly, to be thanking him.

He doubted she would.

What he needed was a shower and a change of clothes. Would that it were as easy to wash away the totally irrational sense of...no, *not* guilt. Why should he feel guilt? If she got hurt the blame lay at her grandfather's door, not his. If she was innocent, she had nothing to fear. He ejected those green eyes from the space in his head that should be occupied by the new addition to the designer label that was about to be incorporated into the Vitale brand. Since the launch of their designer glasses, they had been steadily buying up their rivals. Pretty soon there would be few that were not owned by Vitale.

He had made it halfway to the door before the phone lying on his desk began to vibrate.

He almost ignored it, the call of the fresh set of clothes and shave being strong, but found he couldn't and, when he glanced at the identity of his caller, he was glad he hadn't.

Franco was not only his personal lawyer, he was one of the few people who were privy to the true story of his father's suicide. Of course, the scandal had been big at the time, and was out there in the public arena since yesterday's news. But only a handful of people knew the truth, and Franco was one of them.

He trusted the younger man implicitly and his forensic mind had been invaluable in following the trail of destroyed lives and unravelling the multiple identities of Tor and finally tracking him down.

'Franco…?'

'Are you watching this?'

'Watching what?'

'The latest victim of your revenge… How did it go yesterday? Well, looks like she is involved, or at least the police think so—they're interviewing all the charity trustees. You must be feeling very happy right now. Oh, hell, but this is not a pretty sight. I could almost feel sorry for her.'

'Her who…?' He knew he just wanted to be wrong.

'Anna Randall. Looks like you were right and she *is* guilty, but nothing I found suggested… I know her name is on the board of trustees but she has never attended a meeting and—'

Soren, alert now, his voice urgent, his shower forgotten, cut across his friend. 'What channel?'

'Are you kidding? All of them.'

'Right, stay on the line. I might be needing you.' Soren turned to the images on his laptop screen and unmuted the live feed broadcast.

'These scenes we're watching are of the granddaughter of the disgraced philanthropist Henry Randall, outside the building owned by her grandfather, who is being escorted to the police station, where she is helping with enqui-

ries. People are asking, Tania, how deep does this scandal go? I understand that the sources you have spoken to are denying any government involvement…?'

Soren pressed 'mute' and watched the images on his screen of the modern-day witch trial.

What had Franco said? *Happy?*

Anna, a slim, upright figure dwarfed by the two uniformed figures that flanked her protectively—though not protectively enough to stop her being jostled to the point where she was swamped enough to disappear from view completely at intervals. While the rent-a-mob media crowd—clearly there had been some tip-off—pushed in, firing their inane aggressive questions as they extended their microphones, waving them into her face as she walked, her chin high, displaying the sort of dignified calm under fire that few could have achieved.

Her head didn't go down, she continued to look straight ahead. It was a masterclass in dignity and as he watched her face, the pallor pronounced against the dark chestnut of her hair, he felt his admiration collide with a surge of emotion that he refused to recognise as protectiveness.

Soren swore. This was what he had wanted.

But it so wasn't. He wanted revenge, he wanted justice, but this was not justice and Anna Randall was not his target. Tor should have been standing there, his head bowed in disgrace, not his granddaughter, and even if she was not an innocent, if she was involved at some level, she did not deserve this.

He blanked the screen because, mocked the voice in his head, *You can't see it so it's not happening—and* you *made it happen.*

Innocent or not. Hell, that woman had guts!

He came to a decision.

'Franco, I need you to do something for me...' Soren detailed his requests, his friend and personal lawyer listened.

'So we're helping her? She isn't the enemy?'

An image of Anna Randall flashed into his head...her dark chestnut hair a cloud around her face. She was a woman who disturbed him on more than one level.

'She's a total pain.'

'All right... I see,' said Franco, who didn't. 'OK, give me... I'll get back to you in...just actually don't hang up.'

A few hours previously Anna's only experience of the press was putting an advert in the local paper to ask if anyone had lost a cat, or could give a good home to the six kittens it had given birth to under her bed.

Her only experience of the police was...well,

actually, she didn't have any. Not even a parking ticket. She looked round the anonymous magnolia room, the two chairs on the opposite side of the table, the closed blind on the small high window all adding to the sense of claustrophobia. The only sound was of her knee spasmodically hitting the table; even with both hands pressed to it she couldn't stop the nervous jerking tic.

This was all insane—the police wanted to know how much she knew.

It *should* have been a short conversation—Anna didn't *know* anything—but so far she'd been here two hours. The coffee break suggested she might be here longer. By then, she mused grimly, she might believe she was guilty too.

The first inkling she'd had of the craziness to come was seeing her grandfather's name as she flicked through the news sites before she headed out to treat herself to an outfit for her new job.

International aid agency at the centre of a scandal...accusations of money laundering and facilitating modern slavery!

That was when her phone had started ringing. Journalists asking her for a quote, and others asking her leading questions, such as did she feel guilty that her lifestyle had been funded by the most poor and needy in society?

She had made the mistake of responding a couple of times before someone had repeated her response… "'My grandfather is totally innocent. This is a terrible mistake,'" adding, 'Can I quote you on that?'

When the police had rung she had almost let it ring out, which would, she assumed, have meant the policemen waiting in the car outside would have come knocking on her door, though they had come inside anyway to escort her through the nightmare walk of shame.

She shuddered. Every time she closed her eyes she could still see the flashing lights, and the voices, they were playing in her head like a background white noise. They were the things nightmares were made of…other people's nightmares.

'This is so surreal!' she said to the wall, her commentary cut short when a policeman appeared.

'Can I show you the way out, Miss Randall?'

She jumped and almost knocked her chair over as she leapt like a startled deer to her feet. 'I can go?'

Quick now, Anna, before he changes his mind.

'You know now this is all some terrible mistake!'

The plain-clothes policeman didn't respond to her comment, just looked at her as though he'd heard it all before and from people who were better liars than she was. Was there such a thing as being so innocent you looked guilty?

'Your lawyer has explained the situation,' he said. 'He and your...*friend* are waiting for you.'

Anna hardly noticed the faint hesitation before he said *friend*—she had friends, but she definitely didn't have a lawyer and actually her best friend, Sara, was suffering from a broken heart and had thrown herself into work and moved to Paris. And Penny was looking after her sister's three children while her sister was convalescing from a fall that had left her in plaster.

There was her mum, who was frequently taken for her better-looking, better-dressed big sister, but her mum was *definitely* not the sort of person to stop what she was doing and come to the rescue. The last time she had made contact she had been in another time zone.

It was a real mystery.

The mystery was solved when she stepped past the policeman into an open lobby that was deserted apart from a uniformed senior policewoman who was deep in conversation with a slim young man in a sharp suit who was making her laugh.

Anna barely glanced at them. Her stare had zeroed in on the tall, dramatically dark fallen-angel figure radiating impatience who stood a little apart and was not engaged in the charm offensive.

He was wearing the same things she had seen him in the previous day, but they were now creased, and the tie was gone. His hair was tousled and his jaw and hollow cheeks covered in a dark stubble, that, along with the glitter in his cerulean eyes, added to the combustible charge in the air around him.

He looked dark, dangerous, disreputable and totally in charge.

'You!' She looked around, her hair whiplashing around her face as she searched for the person who was *really* going to rescue her. The odd feeling in the pit of her stomach told her there wasn't going to be anyone else—or something else entirely might be responsible for the *odd* feeling. 'What are you doing here?'

'Cara...finally!'

He was beside her in less time than it took Anna to blink, and she couldn't speak now, her vocal cords were frozen, the glitter in his eyes making her head spin as the long fingers of his right hand slid around the nape of her neck, tilting her face up to him.

He is going to kiss me!

And then he did, a hard, hungry kiss that sent heat pumping through her body and then, without his mouth lifting from hers, the kiss seamlessly expanded to a slow sensual assault on her senses. His mouth, tongue and lips made the journey along her lower lip, tasting and kissing, while he watched her face as she stood, shocked into compliant stillness.

Until stillness was not enough, and she had leaned into him, kissing him back. The abruptness with which he released her made her rock a little on her heels.

Frustration that she was deeply ashamed of clawed low in her belly as, like an automaton, she reacted to the hand in the small of her back guiding her through the big double doors and out into a small courtyard. Her glazed, shocked glance took in her surroundings: some sort of parking area, high walls on three sides; the double gates on the fourth were open.

It was empty apart from one long low limo with blackout windows. As they emerged so did the driver, who walked around to the boot and pulled out a bicycle.

'What are you doing?' *More to the question what am I doing?* 'You kissed me!' she accused.

'You kissed me back.'

She lifted her chin. 'In your dreams!'

Probably, he thought. 'I didn't know what you were about to say, maybe the first thing that came into your head, which might have contradicted to some degree what we had said, so I was giving the nice policeman an explanation that he can accept, otherwise he might have thought I was kidnapping you.'

She resisted the hand lightly placed in the centre of her back, the hand that was guiding her to the limo.

'I think you are.'

'Rescuing you, yes, you can thank me at a later date.'

'Kidnapping me,' she retorted, ignoring the irony as she literally dug her heels in. 'But thank you, though I don't know how or why you are here doing this.'

'You're limping.'

She clamped her lips over a crude retort; he really did destroy her normally very nice manners. 'New shoes. Now, do you mind? I am more than capable of finding my own way home,' she retorted with dignity, trying to remember if she had put her purse in her bag.

'Just get in the car. Do not—what is the saying?—look a gift horse in the mouth.'

She looked at him, careful not to include his mouth in her flash scrutiny. He was no horse, he was a sleek panther...and no one in their right mind got in a car with a feral big cat.

'I am not getting into a car like that with a man I... Oh, yes, you've told me your name, but you could be anyone...a journalist after a story?'

'Now you're thinking like a sensible person.'

Her eyes narrowed. 'Are you admitting you are?'

'No, but you should always assume the worst of people. Cynicism is not a fault, it is a survival essential.'

Perplexed by his logic, she shook her head. 'This has been a very confusing day.'

And she thought it was over? 'You are far too naive to be a successful criminal.' *Though maybe not to be an accomplice...who cared for her grandfather enough to do anything for him?*

'I'm not a criminal, I'm a librarian!' she wailed in frustration, which turned into indignation when he laughed.

His grin faded as he dragged a hand through his hair. 'Get in the car, Anna.'

She thought of that kiss and shook her head, pausing when she heard a distant rumble that she struggled to identify.

The smartly suited young man reappeared. 'Sounds like someone tipped them off we've taken the back entrance. Thanks,' he added, taking the bike from the driver. 'Best way to get through rush-hour traffic,' he said with a grin to Anna. 'Franco, by the way, and sorry we didn't get you out of there sooner,' he said, mounting the bike and adding, 'I'm off, and you might like to not hang around either, Soren, unless you want to make the evening news bulletins?'

Anna watched him ride away. 'He is…?'

'Your lawyer.'

'He looks expensive.'

'He's a friend and he's right, unless you want to meet up with your friends from the press…?'

He watched the shudder of revulsion ripple through her before he turned and walked across to the rear door. His sardonic gaze held hers as he pulled it open while the driver, without a word, jumped into the driving seat.

'Your choice.'

Anna stood there torn with indecision. The noise was getting louder, identifiable now as the babble of approaching voices, with a few laughs and curses thrown in.

Choice—there was no choice… She took a deep breath, and, trying not to favour her painful foot, walked up to the limo, not meeting his eyes as she edged past him to settle inside the luxurious leather-lined interior. She shut her eyes as the door closed behind her.

She opened them again when Soren slid in beside her and experienced a moment of panic as she recalled the searing frustration when he had stopped kissing her and the feeling of being totally out of control that had preceded it.

'This is a nightmare, but I'll be home soon.'

She soothed herself with the facts and refused to think about the kiss.

'Ah...that might not be such a good idea—'

Her green eyes flew wide in panicked protest. 'But—!'

'The press are staked out outside your flat, unless you fancy running the gauntlet?'

He watched her shudder again and deflate and let his sympathy stir.

'Don't worry, alternative arrangements have been made.'

And my compliance is taken for granted. Her eyes narrowed. 'They have?'

He heard the cool in her voice and ignored it; it was less easy to ignore the female scent of her warm skin. 'Yes, it's all in hand, and long-distance walking is not involved.'

She watched as his eyes slid down her slim calves to her narrow ankles and neatly crossed feet.

'What are you staring at?'

Unwilling to admit even to himself that he had lost control of the direction of his gaze, he came back with an exasperated, 'Women and shoes... Why on earth did you put them on if they are crippling you?'

'Oh, I don't know, maybe because the police were waiting for me and I didn't have time to select an outfit that would win your approval.'

At least the cut-off pale blue jeans were comfortable, but she had always felt that the snug fit across her hips only accentuated the boyish narrowness she despised. Normally she would disguise this lack of feminine inches with an oversized shirt or thigh-length tunic, but when the phone had rung she'd been wearing a dip-dye blue sleeveless vest that had shrunk in the wash and revealed slivers of her midriff, a fact she was only just discovering as she now registered a draught around her middle.

She tugged at the hem, but didn't glance down; she knew what she saw would not be confidence-boosting. 'Stop the car!' The decision was so fast she didn't see it coming herself.

'What?'

'I'm not being *arranged* by some random man who says he knows my grandfather.'

He studied her face with an assessing look and folded his hands across his chest. 'Fine, but first things first. Ask away.'

She shook her head. 'What do you mean?'

'You want my credentials, simply ask. I am,' he claimed, spreading his hands in an expansive gesture, 'an open book. Let me start. Well, you already know my name. I am Soren Steinsson Vitale, head of the Vitale Group, which is, as of last year, the largest media company in Europe. We retain an interest in the engineering company my grandfather started up and in specialist steel manufacturing. Shall we leave it at our interests are diverse? You probably have an electrical item in your kitchen that one of our factories made, and the specialised steel in your—'

'I get the idea—you are rich and were born with a golden spoon in your mouth.'

'Not born—the golden spoon was acquired a little later in life and I earned it. I also speak several languages, and I have my own teeth.' He flashed her a mocking, very white smile. 'But I think perhaps you already know this because you must have put my name into a search engine?'

'Because you're so fascinating?' This seemed like an occasion when the truth was the least humiliating option. 'I might have,' she conceded. 'But after you left, my grandfather had an...episode. People in the later stages of dementia often suffer seizures.'

Without warning the tears welled in her eyes and she brushed them angrily away and then gave the same treatment to the hand that was extended towards her. 'I'm fine,' she snarled.

He concealed his concern with a casual shrug; feeling protective towards an attractive woman was something he did not want to get accustomed to. The women in his life all had one thing in common: self-sufficiency. Maybe two: they all shared his pragmatic attitude to sex. Maybe three: they did not expect him to pretend to feel something he did not.

'He's totally innocent, you know. You *do* know that, don't you? The things they are saying. If you knew him like I do… He's always been there for me. When Mum went on one of her adventures he was there. Social services would have issued a care order after I broke my arm when Mum left me with Maggie, but he stepped…' She paused as her voice thickened with emotion. 'It's all a terrible mistake!'

He looked into her earnest emerald eyes and saw a shadow of the little girl who had been passed around because her mother was a selfish bitch. Maybe Tor had done one good thing in his life but that was never going to compensate for the bad things he had done.

'You'd do anything for him, wouldn't you?' he said, wondering what she had done even if she didn't realise it.

'Of course.' She sounded offended that he could ask. 'Ask your father. He knew… Oh, sorry…'

'Your grandfather changed my father's life.'

Oblivious to the undertones, she smiled. 'After the way those policemen were looking at me, you don't know how good it is to actually talk to someone who knows the truth,' she said, feeling her antagonism lowering. It would have been an exaggeration to say she was relaxed. He was not a man she could ever imagine being relaxed around…any man who kissed as he did. She clenched her jaw and firmly closed down the pathway her thoughts were leading her to.

'The truth usually comes out in the end.'

'That's what I think too!'

He looked into the eyes lifted to his, shining with an idealism that she would inevitably lose in the next few days and weeks—and she'd be better for it, or at least more able to survive in the real world.

While he remained reluctant to give anyone related to Tor the benefit of the doubt, it seemed likely that any involvement on her part had been unknowing…but then ignorance was no defence in a court of law.

CHAPTER FOUR

'Isn't that your lawyer?'

Soren nodded as Franco, in the cycle lane, punched the air with triumph as he overtook them, the lane they were in having ground to a slow crawl.

'He is your lawyer,' Soren corrected.

When he had made his request to Franco, his friend hadn't challenged him or asked him why he was doing this, why he was helping Tor's granddaughter, but Soren knew he wanted to.

Anna herself *had* asked him.

Soren was asking himself.

In a rush of unwelcome honesty he likened his own replies to a politician dodging the difficult question and choosing to answer a different one.

Soren was a man who controlled his own destiny. He did not give away that control to regrets or doubts, he set an objective and ruthlessly dismissed anything that interfered with achieving it. Was it a strength or was it a weakness? He didn't know, it was just him—it was the way he dealt with distractions.

Anna Randall sitting beside him would not be dismissed, neither would the sexual vibration between them. He looked at her through the veil of his lashes resenting the fact she could make him feel something he did not want to.

Resenting her and, yes, *wanting* her.

Wanting to punish her for who she was, and wanting to protect her… The conflict simmering inside constantly threatened to boil over at any moment. He felt as if he were walking on eggshells barefoot.

From the moment he had set eyes on her there had been a recognition; he had instantly sensed the fire, the promise of passion that he had wanted to explore.

Tor Randall's granddaughter just wouldn't vacate his head. Innocent or guilty, too attractive for comfort or not, she *was* Tor's granddaughter—that fact alone put her totally off limits.

He faced his uncomfortable facts so why the hell couldn't she? Why could she not see that Tor was as guilty as hell?

What was it going to take to make her see her grandfather for who he was, what he was…?

It frustrated the hell out of him that even after today she seemed to have no real concept of what was coming, no idea of the truth bomb that was about to explode in her face.

Maybe it was something that only those who had lived the experience could appreciate, and he had. He regretted her name would be associated for ever with the breaking scandal, but it was not down to him. He was the catalyst, not the cause.

It was a fact of life that the innocent suffered along with the guilty. She was not his responsibility, and he didn't need the feelings of guilt that were both illogical and uncomfortable. She would have a tough time but she would move on.

His mother hadn't.

He pushed away the thought, focusing instead on the steely core he had sensed in Tor's granddaughter, a resilience that his own emotionally vulnerable parent had never had.

Anna would survive but she wouldn't be the same person sitting beside him. What part of herself would she lose?

Why did the idea bother him?

For the first time in many years Soren found he could not distance himself from his emotions. The acknowledgment infuriated him, but rather than give into those emotions he reached the logical conclusion that the best way to make them go away was to address the cause.

He was going to remove her from the path of

the oncoming storm and after that it was up to her what she did.

He leaned back into the corner of the car, pushing his head against the cream leather padding.

'Relax,' he advised, thinking she was wound so tight that any false move might shatter her like fragile glass.

It seemed to Anna that this was advice he might well follow himself. No wonder she felt fraught—behind his laid-back facade he was so tense it felt like sitting next to an unexploded bomb!

She glanced at his clenched profile through her lashes… Unbidden, her glance drifted to his mouth.

Fighting the urge to touch her own lips, she blurted, 'I am relaxed.'

It was a lie and his sardonic look suggested she was fooling no one.

'And you're not about to throw yourself from a moving vehicle?'

'I wasn't. I would have waited for it to stop. Oh, all right, not relaxed, but it has not been a relaxing day and, besides, my mother told me never to get into cars with strange men.' The flippant addition was a lie, she hadn't, though it was a story Anna had told so often that she almost believed it.

It was one of her selection of *caring parent* stories. She had built up quite a repertoire of them during her school days so that she could roll her eyes along with school friends and join in as they bemoaned how their parents were such pains who had *no idea*!

What would they have said if they had realised that Anna had nobody telling her what to do, that she didn't want to escape, but longed for the security of some restrictions to complain about?

Even on the other side of the world her mum might have seen the headlines; she'd be worried. Her mum might be selfish, but Anna knew she did care for her in her own way.

'What are you doing?'

He watched as she rifled through the contents of the bag she held on her knee like a shield… *against him*? Unfortunately the shield did not totally conceal the sliver of smooth stomach that his eyes kept drifting to… *Was she that smooth and silky all over?*

'I think I forgot my phone.'

'I would imagine you'd know by this point,' he said drily, handing back a lipstick that had rolled against his leg. He didn't miss the fact she made a conscious effort not to touch his fingers, or that her lips were not coated with any of the 'sweet cinnamon' she tucked back into her bag.

'I should get a message to my mum. She will be worried.'

From what Franco's research had revealed about her mother, Soren seriously doubted it.

Married young, widowed young, Mia Randall had decided that parenthood was not for her, though even before she took off for good she had not allowed having a small child to interfere with her adventurous globetrotting lifestyle.

His friend, not normally one to judge, had offered the opinion that some people should not have children.

Soren did not disagree, but he didn't judge so harshly, perhaps because *he* was one of those innately selfish people that children would be better off without.

This was not information he had as yet shared with his grandfather, who frequently spoke of the great-grandchildren he anticipated. There were occasions when he arranged for Soren to *stumble* over eligible mates, and Soren never called him on it, not because he was afraid of conflict with the old man but because he saved those explosive encounters for things that actually mattered to him.

When it came to marriage they were never going to be on the same page. His grandfather, who was obsessed with his *legacy*, would never understand that Soren lived in the present and did not think about the future or care about his legacy. The past had to this point taken up most of his emotional energy, that and achieving some sort of closure.

'Use mine if you like?' he offered casually.

'I... I don't know her number...or, for that matter, if there's any reception where she is.'

'Which is where?'

Her eyes slid self-consciously from his. 'I'm not totally sure. She was in Brazil the last time she made contact.'

'Last time...?'

'It's fine. I'll contact her when I get home... Where are we going?' A glance out of the window told her it was nothing like her north London address. Ambitiously advertised as a penthouse, it was more realistically an attic, a nice attic. The sight of a patch of green through the roof window had swung it for her, along with the fact she could reach two Tube stations in a five-minute walk.

The leafy tree-lined avenue skirting the park they were driving along was several pay grades above where she lived.

'Not far now.'

She glanced sideways, felt her stomach flutter and thought, *Thank God!*

'I still don't... Why are you even here? How

did you know that I was there…at the police station?'

'It was hard not to know. I think most news channels carried the story and the pictures of you leaving your flat. There was also a nice little interview with the taxi driver, who spoke quite movingly of your tears.'

She looked horrified by the information. 'Oh, God! I didn't cry.' A few sniffs did not constitute crying.

'It could have been worse, but apparently you reminded him of his daughter. Is the air conditioning too low? You're shivering—shall I turn it up?'

'No, I'm fine.' Dabbing her tongue at the beads of sweat along her upper lip, she managed a cracked laugh. 'Delayed reaction. I've just never been a police suspect before.' She tried to make it sound like a joke and didn't make it.

He fought the urge to comfort her and masked his concern with a show of abruptness. 'It's their job. It wasn't personal.'

'It felt pretty personal.' She paused, realising that the car had slowed and taken a turn under an arch into a private parking facility.

The longing to be in her own space and lock the door behind her was physical in its intensity. 'When will it be safe to go back to my flat?'

Anna was inclined to risk it, anyway. It wasn't as if he were going to stop her.

He could always kiss her—that had been pretty effective.

The thought came from nowhere and for several seconds her mind went blank as she relived the wild urgency she had experienced before he had closed it down.

He had closed it down!

'I think I should go back to my flat. Surely if I'm so damned infamous…there's nowhere I can hide? There are people in hotels too,' she pointed out. 'Maybe I should run away to Iceland?'

Anna needed her own space. She'd spent the entire day so far putting on a mask for people, trying to prove she was innocent, trying to prove that she was totally cool with breathing the same air as this man.

'Somewhere warmer perhaps?' Soren's gaze ran over the pale contours of her face. Her skin was less creamy warmth and more ghostly pale. Even without the blue smudges emphasised by the shadow of her long lashes there was a bruised quality to her green-eyed gaze.

His scrutiny made her want to cover her face; the impulse made her annoyed with herself all over again.

The car had come to a stop now, but he made no attempt to get out.

'Has no one ever told you it's rude to stare? Or have you never seen a woman without a full face of make-up before?' she grouched.

'Not one that looks like you.'

Their glances held a moment too long, long enough to make her heart thud out of control and put a stomach-quivering question mark in her head, until he continued, his attitude all practicality tinged with something close to boredom that made her feel she was making a big deal out of nothing.

'This isn't a hotel. My mother keeps an apartment here. She rarely uses it.' An expression she struggled to name slid across his face. 'You can stay there until things are settled.'

'You mean until I know if I'm about to be arrested?'

He watched her attempt to make it a joke. Even taking away the quivering lip she clamped down on hard, it would not have convinced a baby, though it did produce a fresh kick of guilt, this time tinged with admiration as the image of her pushing her way through the press pack earlier played in his head on a slow-motion loop.

It took someone with hidden reserves to come out of that sort of thing with dignity, and she had. There must have been some people watching her as she'd looked straight ahead, not reacting to the questions being slung at her like missiles, who had wanted to cheer.

Besides him.

'You've had a bad day, haven't you, *cara*?' His languid delivery almost disguised the concern he resented feeling.

Anna felt her eyes fill with tears and blinked rapidly, trying not to look at the shoulder that was too close and too tempting. 'For God's sake, don't be nice to me,' she demanded through clenched teeth.

Some of the tension left his face as he loosed a laugh. It would seem she required his sympathy even less than he wanted to give it—the more he was around this woman, the more unusual he found her.

The more attractive he found her.

'Don't worry, I can never keep it up. Nature will win out in the end.' His white grin held self-mockery.

'You're not a nice person?' Distracted from her misery, she managed a watery smile.

'They call my grandfather Il Demonio. The Devil,' he translated.

Her brows lifted. It seemed dramatic, but there were people calling her grandfather worse at the moment.

'And you're just a chip off the old block,' she joked tiredly, and she *was* tired. She made a con-

scious effort to allow her rigid spine to flex and
felt relief as her shoulder blades burrowed into
the support of the backrest. The buzz of tension in her head and the knots in her shoulders
were beginning to loosen… It probably wasn't
the right time or place and definitely not the right
company to lower her defences.

'You're not the first person to make that com-
parison.'

Stifling another yawn, she shifted in her seat
to face him full on, her annoyance showing as
she retorted, 'I wasn't and I won't be. I don't care
what your reputation is, I judge people from their
actions. You visited an old sick friend of your
father, and you are here now, helping me. Even
though you don't know me and despite the fact
being seen with me will probably taint you by
association… Will it?' she shot out anxiously.

His lips quirked. 'I will survive.'

'And so far I have not been very grateful. I
happen to think you are very kind.' And his actions went way beyond normal *kindness*.

Soren opened the door and stepped out. Guilt
seemed to be becoming his factory setting.

To ward off the feelings as he walked around
to open her door, he reminded himself that the
guilt was not his. *He* was not the villain of this
situation. Tor Rasmusson was.

A fact that was hard to cling to when her

white-faced gratitude was making him feel as guilty as hell. Frustration made his jaw ache. Obviously he regretted that she, *anyone* inno-cent, if she was, had been caught up in this, but he wasn't about to regret it.

He wasn't sorry, he told himself, ignoring the contradictory fresh kick of remorse, and there were a whole lot of victims out there who might get some recompense now.

Not apologise, but for a brief moment he toyed with the notion of telling her the truth.

He discarded it almost immediately, even though it would be guaranteed to wipe the ide-alistic glow from her eyes, which quite frankly would have been a relief.

It was many years since Soren had needed the good opinion of others; his hesitation now was a matter of practicality.

She wasn't ready to accept the truth about her grandfather, although it would be better for her when she did. But he was well aware that the mo-ment he came clean and revealed that he himself was the architect of her grandfather's downfall he would immediately become a monster in her eyes, which was fine by him. He'd been called worse before and often by his own grandfather.

Soren had a very thick skin.

CHAPTER FIVE

'I'M JUST SO glad that I'm not the only one who knows Grandpa Henry is innocent,' she said as she exited the limo with a degree of poise, if not elegance. She was just congratulating herself on that when she dropped her bag and the contents spilt out and began rolling away across the concrete floor of the garage.

Maybe he was a monster...maybe he'd spent too long trying to think like a monster. The pursuit of his quarry over all these years had involved inserting himself into Tor's mindset. Had he become the thing he'd been hunting?

Silencing the inner dialogue, Soren frowned. This wasn't about him; he had nothing to justify. What had he been meant to do? Pat the guy on the back and say, 'All is forgiven, don't do it any more'?

He hadn't been looking for justice for the masses when he'd outed Tor Rasmusson, but they had it anyhow and he had his revenge.

'Can you manage?' he said, unable not to enjoy the view of her tight little bottom.

'Almost,' she said, responding to the impatience in his voice as she chased the last errant item from her bag, which had rolled under a sports car... The extra stretch to reach it caused her top to ride up a little higher, revealing a section of her lower back that no one with testosterone could have missed.

Smooth and pale, her skin had a satiny appearance; he had no way of testing his theory that it would feel like oiled silk without touching it.

He dragged his eyes clear but not before his imagination had supplied a number of scenarios that involved touching, with his hands, his lips... He pushed away the image of her body arching to his touch while he anchored her hips to the... He cleared his throat and reached for the control panel to his right and was relieved when the overhead air conditioning kicked in, flooding the immediate area with an icy blast of air.

She got to her feet. 'The zip is broken.'

'You do know, don't you, that *my* opinion is not the one that matters? It's about proof.'

Anna wasn't sure if her shiver this time was in response to the ice in his voice or the sudden drop in temperature. She closed the zip and tugged it experimentally; it held.

'I don't need proof. I *know*...'

Her calm conviction as she smiled serenely up at him drove him closer to the edges of his self-control. *Nobody* could be that stupid and blind!

'The law relies on facts, not feminine intuition.'

And they had plenty of facts, Soren knew. He had supplied a forensically detailed file that had been forwarded to the police: the list of victims, the varied aliases, and the money. It always followed the money, a lot of it locked away in offshore accounts.

Something in his tone made her glance sharpen on his face. There was nothing to see there beyond the startling perfection, the harmony and strength of angles and planes. Even bone-tired in body and mind she reacted to that beauty…and her feminine intuition was yelling *danger*…

He watched as she gave her head a tiny shake, dragging some rich dark strands of hair from her face and raising her arms to combine them briefly at the nape of her neck, the action lifting her narrow ribcage and emphasising her slim, supple curves.

There was something almost feline about her streamlined body. She made zero effort to be provocative; in fact, as impossible as it seemed to him, she seemed oblivious to the innate sensuality she exuded.

'I'm being realistic, not emotional, all right, I am being emotional but—' She sighed. 'This is all so... Well, at least they can't send him to prison. He's already there. If he wasn't he would be able to clear his own name—' she snapped her fingers '—just like that.' Anna fell into step beside him. 'He can't, so I will.' She wasn't quite sure how yet, but she was pretty sure it would be harder if she were sitting in a prison cell herself.

Soren slowed his pace to accommodate the difference in their stride and the fact she was limping.

'We'll take the lift,' he said in response to her questioning look as they passed the staircase. 'When was the last time you ate?'

It was a masterful change of subject. 'I don't know.'

'Eat, then talk strategy.'

She sighed. 'All right.'

The glass-sided lift whooshed silently to the top of the building. She was in a lift with a man who must be regarded as dangerous by any woman under ninety and she was safe—he was not looking at her, or the multiple reflections of her in the walls, but at his phone. God, it was so depressing!

Not that she wanted to have to fight him off, but just a little frisson of possibility would have made her feel more like a...woman. *Sure, be-*

cause there's nothing that makes you feel more like a woman than fighting a man off in a lift.

Would you be fighting?

Soren waited until she had exited the lift before he emerged. The scent of her perfume in the enclosed space had been driving him crazy.

'This way...'

She entered a little ahead of him.

'This is very...' She looked curiously round the loft-style open-plan space; it was like a photo shoot for a glossy magazine. Minimalist and expensively impersonal. She chose the room's selling point. 'Lovely view.' One wall was glass and looked out over the river.

He wasn't looking at the room; he had been looking at her behind and now he was scrutinising her legs. His expression did not suggest admiration.

'First, we sort that foot.'

'It's fine,' she said, trying not to wince as she stamped her foot down to prove her point. While she'd been in the police station adrenaline and panic had blurred any pain, but now her screaming nerve endings were making themselves felt.

'Take it off.' Their eyes clashed and he added drily, 'Your shoe.'

'I won't be able to get it back on.'

He arched a sardonic brow and looked bored. 'And that is a bad thing why?'

She sighed and limped across to one of the immaculate crease-free sofas. Lowering herself onto it, she bent her leg and slowly peeled off the offending shoe, before settling back with a sigh and stretching her throbbing foot out in front of her.

There was a grimace of distaste on her face as she tilted her foot from side to side to see the offending area.

'I think the blister might have burst.' There was no think about it; it was a mess.

'What are you doing?'

'I don't want to get blood on your sofa.' Actually, the rug was white too.

He swore and placed a hand on her shoulder as she struggled to her feet, or at least one of them. At the last minute, overbalancing, she fell back with a grunt.

She slung him an indignant look.

'I have no idea why women put themselves through agony for the sake of fashion.'

The hypocrisy! 'Does it never occur to you that the almost-dressed women hanging onto your arm are doing so to stop falling over?'

'How do you know I have women hanging on my arm?'

'A wild guess?' she suggested sourly. Another educated guess was they would all possess endless legs and perfect faces.

'Why buy shoes that don't fit?'

'They were a bargain.'

He looked genuinely bemused by the explanation but then she didn't imagine he did much bargain-hunting.

'Let me see.'

She retracted her leg. 'Why?'

He rolled his eyes. 'So I can post a photo on— Why the hell do you think? So I can see the damage.'

'It's nothing.'

He sighed and looked bored again, or at least bored with a clenched ticcing jaw. 'Spare me the brave-little-soldier attitude and let me see!'

She felt his gaze for a moment before she threw up her hands. 'All right.' Hands clasped supportively under her thigh, she lifted her leg and wriggled her toes, a mistake, it hurt, before retracting her foot and throwing out a childish, 'Happy now?'

The provocation of her pout took him a moment to move beyond.

His touch was clinical and light around her slender ankle as he turned her extended foot to view the damage.

What he saw made him swear. 'It's a mess.'

'And I always thought my feet were one of my selling points.'

Her attempt at humour did not go down well.

'You've made it worse walking around on it.'

'I spent most of the time sitting down being grilled. I didn't really notice until… It's only a blister. I really don't see what you're making a fuss about.'

He swore again. It was Italian-sounding, and with his carved features set in a scowl he looked very brooding—Latin with a side order of Viking thrown in. In short, very gorgeous.

'What about the other foot?'

'That's not too bad,' she husked, the tenderness in her foot no longer the problem. It was the tingling imprint of his light touch that was bothering her…more than a little. 'I don't think the skin is broken on that one.'

'Think or know.'

'Know,' she said firmly.

'Well, that is going to need cleaning and dressing.'

'I'll get it done when I get home.' She had already decided that she couldn't stay here. She wanted more than ever to go home, by cover of darkness if that was what it took.

'You'll probably have gangrene by then. Wait there!'

He delivered the addition as if it had never occurred to him that anyone would not follow his edicts. She mimed a mocking salute at the retreating back of the man who seemed determined to take over her life.

And she was letting him!

'Oh, God!' she sighed out before sliding back into the showroom-smooth white sofa. Like everything, it looked as though it had never been touched, let alone used.

She swung her legs down to the floor, careful not to jar her foot, and guiltily dusted the pristine fabric before, from her semi-recumbent position, gazing around the very white room, well, multiple shades of white. The effect was actually quite soothing.

Except she was past soothing.

She sat there, her head spinning as the day's events came crowding in, playing like a film on a loop—a horror film.

By the time Soren reappeared she felt as though her head was going to explode with the whirling chaos of disconnected thoughts.

But she clung to the only positive: her grandfather was innocent of what they accused him of. Was she being naive thinking that in the end the truth would always come out?

In the meantime, she had to deal with being one of the central figures in the scandal of the moment, and no one seemed to believe she knew nothing.

As much as she appreciated this offer of a

night's respite, she could not see the point of delaying the inevitable and, although she hated the idea of the press intrusion, someone needed to be out there standing up for Grandpa Henry.

She watched as Soren placed a first-aid box on a side table and pulled it across to the sofa.

'It's very kind of you to offer me a place to stay tonight, but I can't hide for ever.'

He didn't respond to her despondent addition, just looked at her through the half-lowered veil of his dark lashes for a moment longer before grabbing a footstool.

'What if you could?' he said, straddling the stool. 'Hide. Not for ever, but for... Come on...'

In response to his imperative gesture, she lifted her foot and extended it warily towards him. 'Could hide?' she queried, closing her mouth over a shocked sigh as his cool fingers grasped her ankle and yanked it onto his knee.

'Until things die down.' His eyes rose from his contemplation of her foot.

She lifted her chin. 'I'm not going to run away. I haven't done anything wrong. Grandpa has not done anything wrong. I want to tell people that.'

Dio, he thought, imagining her standing there facing a camera while she defended the old bastard. They would crucify her with the realities.

She shifted a little against the white upholstery as his inscrutable bright eyes brushed her face for a moment longer before he bent over the small foot that lay on his knee.

'Your grandfather is safe—his condition not only makes him effectively immune from prosecution, but immune to public opinion.'

'This is about his reputation, not— Ouch!' she yelled.

'Hold still.' He appeared unsympathetic to her pain, but his touch as he continued to dab the raw area with antiseptic was gentle, and as clinical as his manner. 'I'll put a dry dressing on.' She gave another gasp, this time soft, and when he looked up her teeth were digging into her full lower lip, and she was pale, the dark stain along her cheekbones emphasising that pallor. 'You all right?'

Closing her eyes was Anna's only defence against his penetrative stare and the horrifying possibility he had guessed that her gasp was not connected with her blistered foot but the casual brush of his finger along the sensitive skin of her instep.

'Fine, just get on with it…' She softened her abrupt response with a guilty, 'Thank you.'

The belated polite addition drew his eyes back to her face but Anna, who had kept her eyes scrunched closed, did not see.

'It's going to be painful for a while,' Soren warned, thinking that there was a lot of it about, as he continued to focus his effort on ignoring the pain he was feeling, courtesy of the heavy, hot weight of arousal, the killing pressure in his groin.

'It's fine.' She shook her head and opened her eyes, carefully avoiding his. 'I'm finally getting an opportunity to test out all those relaxation apps.' She needed a lot more than a lavender candle, she reflected, wondering when all the self-control had gone from her life.

Relax—that was one thing that Soren couldn't allow himself to do at that moment. He could not afford even temporary hormonal amnesia.

He liked sex.

He liked women.

But, despite his reputation, there was no string of broken hearts, a few bruised egos possibly, but he had no interest in hurting women, and he could smell vulnerable a mile off. Luckily he was attracted to women who were, not just beautiful, but independent, who didn't equate good sex with a meeting of souls.

In Anna Randall's case her vulnerable aura was like a walk in a warm meadow, the sort that made you want to lie down… *She* smelt like a walk in a warm meadow and he had wanted to lie down with her from the moment he saw her. Actually, lying down was purely optional—any angle would have been fine with him so long as he could sink into her.

Obviously he wasn't going to, and not just because she lit up the big red keep-clear lights in his head. He couldn't allow himself to forget *who* she was—this situation was already complicated enough without him sleeping with his enemy's granddaughter.

Soren took a firm grip of his wayward imagination, deleting the tormenting image of her stretched out on the sofa beneath him with her long hair spread out around them. He continued to deliver a monotone running commentary on what he was doing as he applied a light dressing to the raw area.

'Anna, I said is that too tight?'

His voice sounded to Anna as though it were coming from a long way off. She heard the words but didn't react to them. He had not released her foot; his fingers were moving along the curve of her arch slowly and then back again…over and over… She swallowed hard and clenched her lips over a whimper. The touch had started as soothing and moved into totally uncharted territory.

Who even knew there were so many nerve endings under the skin there? And each one was alive, connecting with other nerve endings; the surface layer of every inch of her skin was tingling. Cheeks flushed hot against her pale skin, her head fell back… This time nothing would stop the almost whimper, a broken sound that she could not immediately associate with herself.

She could hear the sound of the sea, only it wasn't; it was, she realised, her own blood pounding in her ears.

She heard him swear. It was the hook she clung onto to drag her free of the deep drowning sensual thrall she was entangled in.

Stop drifting.

'I think…' But she didn't think, she couldn't. His eyes were so deep, drowning blue, bright and fierce, and she was… She swallowed hard and tried to adopt the expression of someone who knew what their name was…what they were doing.

'Anna…' He breathed her name, making it half warning but also strange and exciting. Under the heat in his eyes she sensed a bewilderment as deep as her own and a ferocity that she found unbearably exciting.

Without him breaking eye contact, his fingers moved higher up the curve of her bare calf then higher under the fabric as he reeled her in, pulling until her bottom was on the very edge of the sofa.

Her heart pounded out a heavy beat, until she was barely breathing.

His intense magnetism seemed to be exerting a physical pull. She found herself leaning in; he was leaning in. She recognised the moment they reached a tipping point, but not who made the final move that connected their mouths.

The heat that flared was instantaneous, the combustion seeming to consume the oxygen in the room as the slow, shatteringly sensuous exploration deepened.

The whimper was hers, the groan was his, the rest was lost in a hot blur. Then into the heat haze a noise: the vibration of a phone.

Soren, dark streaks cresting his cheekbones, swore and turned away, rising to his feet and presenting his back to her as he stared at the screen. He swore again, slid it back into his pocket and waited a moment before turning.

'I wouldn't have let you…it…go any…' she blurted, trying not to think about the clash of teeth, the collision of tongues.

His shrug could not have been more languid. 'Sometimes sex is not a bad way to relax after a tough day.'

Her jaw dropped. He made it sound like an option such as a stiff drink or a run in the park—for him it probably was—and it wasn't that she disapproved of his attitude—in fact, on one level, she almost envied him—but she knew that sex for her could never be the casual transaction that it was for him. She knew herself well enough to know that she wanted more, she needed more;

there was no way she could separate her emotions from the physical act.

She wanted that intimacy, she wanted to feel that close to another person, but she was also wary of the wanting, for wanting *too* much. She didn't need to see a therapist to work out she was wanting what she had never had.

But her *fear* had always been greater than her *want*.

She hated that in her; she hated that, even though she had grown into a confident, capable young woman, when it came to her love life there was still that little girl who hadn't been special enough, pretty enough for her own mum to stick around.

Did that even make sense? Anna had no idea.

It was as though the craving for love and the deep-seated fear of rejection were constantly battling inside her.

'I think I should be going home,' she said stiffly.

'No, you stay here, I will go, but first... I have an idea.' Something about his casual tone made her think it wasn't. 'You wanted somewhere to hide?'

'You said that—'

A hissing sound of exasperation left his lips. 'I know you want to battle the forces of evil and clear your grandfather's name—'

The way he said it all snide and snarky brought an angry flush to her face.

'He is an innocent man.'

He gave a sigh. 'This is out of your hands, you must see that?' The stubborn set of her chin suggested she wasn't ready to see anything and certainly not sense.

'Just stay here tonight.'

'This is your mother's home—'

He dismissed the objection out of hand. 'The fact is my mother has never been here. I bought the place hoping that... Not one of my best ideas... Look at that view!'

His comment bemused her; the view was worth several million. 'It's beautiful!'

'Not if you're agoraphobic.' It was a classic example of outsourcing the wrong thing. He had just signed the agent's cheques and hired the most expensive interior designer who had put in a bid—not the one who said she needed to meet the person who would be living here before she accepted the job.

So he got expensive white and glass!

'Oh!' Her eyes went from the wide expanse of glass to his face. 'That's spaces and—'

'That's not being able to step through your front door. My father's death impacted her mental health and...but you really don't want to hear this. Now, my proposal.'

'I don't want to hide.'

'Then let's just think of it as a temporary stepping away, a working holiday.'

Despite herself, she was intrigued. 'Working…?'

'My great-grandfather, over his lifetime, accumulated a rather impressive library, some important manuscripts and various…well, I believe that the word unique has been used to describe it, but the last time anyone with any knowledge of the subject saw it was in the sixties. My grandfather has been talking about cataloguing it for years. Last year he tasked me with it, and I haven't got around to doing anything about it yet.' He studied her face. 'I see I have your attention.'

'That sounds like an incredible opportunity for someone.'

'How about you?'

He was offering her the professional gig of a lifetime. Did he even realise it? 'That isn't possible. My grandfather—'

'Does not even recognise you.'

The brutal truth made her flinch.

'*He* is safe and I am sure he would want to think of you being safe too?' He arched a brow. 'Am I right, he would want the best for you, to protect you?'

'I can protect myself. Where, as a matter of interest, is the library?'

'A rather ancient palazzo in Sicily.'

'Sicily!' she yelped and chuckled. 'I couldn't go to Sicily. My grandfather—'

'Should he need you, it's a very short flight away and Sicily is not the moon. We have running water, fibre connection, and—'

'You live there?'

'Is that a selling point?'

Thinking of the kiss that was never going to happen again, she looked away, regaining her composure before she stuck her chin out and met his gaze head-on with an 'I dare you to disbelieve me' glare. 'It is idle curiosity.'

'I agree it is never a good idea to accept an offer until you know the full job description and conditions—'

'I'm not considering,' she said, a frown forming on her brow when she heard the almost wistful note in her voice. In her defence, it was the sort of job that anyone with expertise would have given a lot for.

Too much to hope he hadn't noticed; Anna doubted anything much escaped him.

'Let's cut to the chase,' he drawled. 'Yours will not involve having sex with me.'

The breath left her chest in one startled gasp;

indignant colour flew to her cheeks. 'I never imagined it would!'

There was nothing caressing about his smile, which weirdly echoed the same self-contempt that gleamed in his heavy-lidded eyes. 'You have a very…limited imagination, *cara*.'

Anna decided to stop digging this particular hole, which was already way past her head. 'You can save the big sell. I'm not considering the offer. I can't leave my grandfather and I already have a job offer at one of the most prestigious university libraries in the country.'

'A job offer is not a job,' he corrected smoothly.

'Actually, it is,' she retorted. 'I start next week.'

'I know enough to know that the likelihood of the job offer vanishing is extremely high. You are associated with a scandal that—'

She pressed a hand to her stomach, feeling sick but defiant. 'You're suggesting I'm toxic,' she quivered out.

'I'm saying that your name is trending and not in a good way. Employers are cautious.'

'But not you,' she snapped, trying to sound as though her entire future had just got significantly worse. 'Sorry,' she tacked on with a grimace. 'I have no idea why I'm being so nasty to you. You're trying to help.'

His eyes slid from hers. Considering that

many—including her—might deem him the author of the situation she was in, the irony of her gratitude was not lost on him. Each fresh reminder, each non- judgmental glance from her clear green eyes, delivered a fresh scratch of guilt to his armour.

'If you'll let me.'

She'd let him kiss her. She'd actively contributed to the kiss.

She pushed the thought away. He clearly considered kissing and what it led to in much the same way she thought of a nice meal and a glass of wine—enjoyable but instantly forgettable.

Which was fine, because Anna had no intention of joining his list of *forgettables* even had the opportunity been on offer.

CHAPTER SIX

'This isn't a tentative offer. I've already handed in my notice.' The local library job had only ever been a stopgap after she had fallen victim to the financial belt-tightening and reorganisation at the boarding school where she had been happy, if unchallenged.

She was way overqualified for the job, but she had never needed her grandfather's help financially and she hadn't been about to start, which turned out to be lucky now all his bank accounts, including the ones she had power of attorney over, were frozen.

'Look, I appreciate the offer, but the job is locked in,' she returned, crossing her fingers. Without a job, even if she didn't end up in jail, she could end up owing money.

'Do you have a signed contract?'

'Not yet,' she admitted, adding defiantly, 'I don't think it's a bad thing to give people the benefit of the doubt. Following that logic…are you saying I shouldn't trust you?'

Which, of course, she wouldn't have if she had been six feet with curves and legs that went on for ever and not five four, with legs that matched and the curves of a coat hanger. She might have been worried or flattered or both, but the kiss that had rocked her world had been for him the equivalent of a stress buster after a bad day.

He hadn't kissed her as if he didn't know she was a woman…

'Have it your way.'

'I will,' she assured him serenely.

'Anna.'

'This is *my* problem.'

'The problem is you don't think there is one. If there is anything that gets more hits or sells more copy than a monster, it's a victim.'

The cynical suggestion aroused Anna enough to protest indignantly despite being close to co-matose with fatigue. 'I am not a victim!'

'I'm not here to debate semantics, but to offer a practical and mutually beneficial solution to your problems.'

Anna rubbed a hand across the tight muscles in her neck and slowly lifted her chin from her chest, where it had dropped, to look at him. On one level she was aware that being able to appreciate the strong, chiselled lines of his amazing

face when her life was falling apart said something about her; she didn't push further down
that particular road of self-analysis.

'This will die down,' she said, willing him to
agree and growing angry when he didn't. 'There
will be another scandal.'

'Sure, riding out the storm is an option…but
why put yourself through that if you don't have
to? And you being here and valuable to any long
lens is just going to feed the interest, prolong it.'

She sat down with a bump as her legs suddenly folded.

Her eyes closed, she sensed rather than heard
him move away.

'Brandy.'

'I'm already falling over.'

'Because you've not eaten, but don't worry,
the food should be here soon.'

'What food?'

'I ordered takeout when we arrived, supper
from the Grove.'

'The Grove as in *the* Grove?' The multi-Mi-
chelin-starred restaurant had a mile-long waiting list of celebrities who wanted to say they
had dined there; also she understood the food
was good.

He nodded.

'They don't do takeout…' She stopped—
maybe they did if you were Soren Vitale. With-

out thinking, she picked up the glass and took a swallow of the contents, the glance she threw him carrying the same defiance as the gesture, and then spoilt it by choking.

'I don't like spirits,' she said hoarsely, but the warm feeling was a lot better than the taste.

'Take it slowly.'

The concern that roughed the edges of his dark bitter-chocolate voice brought an unaccountable lump to her throat. Embarrassed by her over-reaction, Anna nodded and lowered her lashes to shield herself from his disturbing blue stare.

The alcohol had made her panic recede a fraction, but it had also lowered her emotional barrier. What she needed was her own bed and to cry herself to sleep in the dark.

'This is all so surreal. I keep thinking I'm going to wake up.'

'My advice—'

'I know what your advice is.'

'Being here and available,' he reiterated, 'will just fuel the story.'

'Me not being here would not make the police happy.'

'That will not be a problem. You have a good lawyer.'

She shook her head. 'He's not my lawyer, he's *your* lawyer. You are being so kind to me…'

Her voice broke as the emotion totally occluded her throat.

'So you will take the job?'

'I didn't say that,' she protested, thinking this was going way too fast.

'Well, when you do… I'm flying back tomorrow, so if—'

'Tomorrow?' She was startled at the suggestion.

He arched a sardonic brow. 'Would that be a problem?'

She laughed. He sounded surprised by the possibility. 'Yes, actually it is, or it would be if I said yes, which,' she added quickly, 'I'm not.'

'In what way a problem?'

Her brow furrowed deeper. God, he didn't lack persistence, she had to say that much for him.

'Do you never give up? All right, you want a problem, how about I have what I'm standing up in?' She held her arms wide to invite his inspection, patting herself down to demonstrate there were no secret compartments.

There were, however, two shallow pockets in her jeans and one had a phone bulge.

'What is it?'

She wriggled her fingers into the offending pocket and pulled them out with her phone. 'It was here all along.'

'So, about tomorrow…?'

She sighed. 'Do you do everything at this speed?'

His dark lashes swept down; when they lifted a moment later the glow in the cerulean depths made her stomach flip.

'Not everything,' he said, utterly expressionless.

It was several slow-moving moments before her breathless-sounding response dropped into the tense stillness that followed his words.

'I need time to think.' Not about the things happening below waist level—actually, thinking was exactly what she *didn't* need.

'Do you have your passport.'

Her teeth clenched as he continued to act as if her capitulation were inevitable.

'Do you have a tick list or something? Yes, I have my passport. The police wanted it, to check I'm me, I suppose, or maybe they thought I was about to skip the country...' Her green gaze slowly lifted and she shook her head less firmly than she would have liked. 'I have no clothes, not even a toothbrush.'

'Then no problem. I have an account at Harvey Nicks. Tell me what you need and I'll order it.'

'I couldn't do that!' she exclaimed, sounding shocked.

'Why not? I have bought women's clothes before.'

She felt the heat climb to her cheeks. 'I am not one of *your women*,' she retorted.

The dangerous gleam in his eyes made her stomach flip but before it could go anywhere outside her active imagination the intercom buzzed.

Soren said something that sounded Italian under his breath and stalked across to the intercom discreetly set in the wall.

'The food is here.'

'I just need the...?'

'Second door on the left.' He nodded in the direction.

She spent a few minutes in the bathroom, too emotionally whacked to take much pleasure from the luxury fixtures and fittings.

She felt marginally better after washing her hands and face, although one glance told her that her hair was beyond rescue. She put on some lipstick, found it made her look even more ghostly and clashed with the blue shadows under her eyes, and wiped it off again.

Back in the open-plan living area the table by the window had been laid; the dimmed lights emphasised the dramatic night-lit skyline beyond. The overall effect was romantic.

So long as you don't forget it isn't, Anna.

He held out a chair and she limped across to take it.

'If I'd known, I would have dressed for dinner.' She scanned the table with some appreciation. It might be a takeaway but not as she knew; the food on the table was served on white porcelain and slate.

'I asked for a light supper.'

'It looks so pretty!' she exclaimed. 'A work of art.'

He looked amused. 'Let us hope it tastes as good.'

He went to fill her glass from the bottle in the cooler and she frowned. 'I probably shouldn't.'

'You should do something you probably shouldn't at least once a day.'

'My mum would approve of that philosophy. This is delicious. I can't figure out what is in this sauce...'

'It's pretty well disguised,' Soren, whose own taste ran to simpler food, commented as he sat back watching her, enjoying her enthusiasm and her unselfconscious appreciation of the food. 'But you don't approve of doing something you shouldn't?'

'Oh, I'm boring. I have no spirit of adventure, Mum says. Poor Mum, she was expecting her daughter to be like her, or at least to be pretty. It came as a nasty shock when I told her I wanted to be a librarian. Her face... I honestly think she'd have been less shocked if I said I wanted to be a sex worker!' She laughed, her gaze lifting a little self-consciously from her plate when he didn't respond.

'Is something wrong?' she asked when she discovered he looked unaccountably stern, angry even. 'I babble when I drink,' she said, putting down the glass she had just picked up.

'I like your voice.'

It seemed an odd thing to say.

'Do you not like the wine?'

'It's gorgeous. Everything is gorgeous,' she said, looking across the table. There were acres of food left over, which seemed a criminal waste. Her grandfather's housekeeper, who had been her female role model growing up, had instilled a frugality in her. 'But I really couldn't eat another scrap.'

'There is pudding in the fridge.'

His teasing offer made her groan and press both hands to her stomach. 'I couldn't...' she admitted regretfully. 'Your driver—has he had any food?'

'Considerate, but I sent Alberto home a while ago.'

'Then how...? Oh, a taxi,' she realised.

'Actually, I'm staying here tonight.'

As his casual bombshell dropped and the ripples of comprehension spread, Anna's glass hit the table with a bump. She barely registered it slopping all over the surface.

'Why?' she exclaimed, then flushed. 'Not that it's any of my business.' This was his house, or his mother's, which amounted to the same thing, *she* was the guest and she was massively over-reacting.

'I do not sleepwalk, if that is what is concerning you.'

The taunt seemed unnecessarily cruel to Anna, who might have spent most of her time in the bathroom *avoiding* looking at her reflection, but she had seen enough to know that this was sarcasm. Soren could have his pick, and she was sure that a man like him would be very picky—everything about him came with an *only supermodel-level females or above need apply* sticker.

And they, she decided—thinking long legs and inflatable breasts—were welcome to him.

'It isn't!' she said, channelling cold towards his veiled eyelids. 'Sorry if I'm boring you,' she added when he didn't react.

'Also I am a light sleeper.' Though he seriously doubted that the night would bring him any sleep at all. 'So if you have any plans to slip away in the night…'

Anna had forgotten those plans somewhere around her second glass of wine.

'I'll go home tomorrow,' she said in a flat little voice.

'What are you doing?'

Anna stopped stacking plates. 'Clearing the—'

'Go to bed, Anna. You are the guest.'

Escape seemed a better option than arguing or suggesting he didn't know how to stack a dishwasher.

'Last door on the right,' he said in response to her questioning look.

'Right, then, goodnight.'

'Sleep well, Anna,' he called after her.

Anna didn't expect to sleep at all. Maybe it was the room's cool Scandi-blonde vibe or her total exhaustion, but she slept a solid dreamless seven hours and woke wondering where she was.

The blissful amnesia didn't last long. Rolling out of bed, she sat on the edge—she had slept in her bra and panties—and hid her face in her hands for a full indulgent thirty seconds before she remembered she had never got around to contacting her mum.

No one picked up, not exactly a shock, so she left a text before having a look to see what was going on in the world. Only to discover she was!

She was reeling from the level of her exposure when she noticed the missed calls and the texts.

The university expressed great regret, but

they apparently had a duty of care to their students and their reputation to consider so, after due consideration, they had decided to rescind their offer.

It took her a few moments to overcome the waves of nausea before she was able to grab the robe from behind the door. Still tying it, she headed straight to the living area where Soren, wearing a towel wrapped around his middle, was drinking coffee.

Shock nailed her to the spot as she took in his broad shoulders, the deeply tanned, perfect, lean musculature of his torso, his long hair-roughened legs and impressive powerful thighs.

All he needed was a mythical hammer, and he could have been mistaken for the Viking god who wielded it.

'Oh, no!' she groaned. Shock seemed to have temporarily paralysed the self-censoring area of her brain. 'Get some clothes on, please!'

'Good morning, Anna.'

There not being an option of a convenient black hole opening up at her feet, she ignored the sardonic mockery in his voice and the wicked gleam in his heavily lidded eyes.

'Is the job offer still there?'

His grin vanished, replaced by a hard calculating look. 'It is.'

'Good, then I'll take it. Oh, and, yes, you were

right: no job. Apparently I am a danger to stu-dents!' She gave a shrill little bitter laugh. 'But I need to speak with the clinic first, and the offer of clothes—order a few and I'll pay you back for them.'

His lips twitched. 'I'll take it from your first pay cheque,' he promised.

'But the flight, will there be time…?'

'The new wardrobe will arrive in…ten min-utes.'

'You knew I'd change my mind,' she accused.

'I was confident that you would see the advan-tages of the arrangement,' he corrected smoothly. 'Help yourself to coffee, the croissants are still warm, and I will go to put some clothes on.'

By the time Anna had showered a pile of boxes and bags lay on her bed along with a set of empty designer cases.

She stood there staring at them, shocked at the sheer quantity—this was no one's idea of a capsule wardrobe—while Soren yelled through the closed door.

'Just pick out something for travelling and dump the rest in the cases,' he suggested. 'I need to attend to a few things. Alberto will pick you up and bring you to the airport. Oh, and, Anna, he has instructions not to take you to the clinic even if you beg. The press have the place staked out.'

Did anyone ever say no to him? she wondered, tipping the contents of one of the bags onto the bed. The slither of colourful silk turned out to be several matching bra and panties sets...in the right size.

As the pile of items grew it became clear that there was more than a year's salary worth of designer clothes lying there, including two ball gowns that were not something a librarian wore, and she hadn't got to the line of shoeboxes yet.

CHAPTER SEVEN

NORMALLY TAKE-OFF WAS a big thing for Anna, and not in a good way. More of a white-knuckle, take-a-deep-breath way. She did close her eyes and take a stranglehold grip of the arm rests of her seat, but there was too much going on in her head to allow for outright gibbering panic.

It wasn't just the novelty of being on a private flight that distracted her.

She was wondering where Soren was, and if the driver had told him she had tried to persuade him to take her to the clinic. As she had pointed out in her attempts to coax him, it was *almost* on the way.

It had seemed worth a try and she hadn't said she *wouldn't* say goodbye to Grandpa. Soren, in his typical overbearing style, had just taken her compliance as a given.

If Soren said anything she'd tell him that she didn't owe him any explanations, she wasn't working for him yet. Actually, it wasn't his reaction that occupied her thoughts, it was her grand-father. She knew he was being well cared for and the likelihood was he really wouldn't notice her absence, but it still felt like running away.

And Anna had never been the sort of person who ran away, *until now*…because, though you could dress it up any way you chose, she *was* running away, taking the easy way out and aban-doning her grandfather.

Tears of self-disgust stung closed eyelids as she felt the plane level smoothly off.

'You going to spend the entire journey with your eyes closed?'

The soft, slightly mocking voice made Anna's eyes snap open, wide, wary and probably, she re-alised with a sinking heart, providing evidence that just the sight of him sitting opposite, his long legs stretched out under the table between them, was enough to send her sensitive stomach muscles into a steep spiralling dive.

She'd heard it said that sexual attraction was something you couldn't rationalise; she now knew it was true. They also said it was some-thing you couldn't control but Anna refused to believe that. She thought of that kiss and really hoped her conviction was never put to the test… She ignored the kick of excitement in her pelvis as she thought about the consequences of failing.

Feeling like someone fighting their way out

of a deep hole of their own making, she forced a smile, cleared her throat and, mentally at least, squared her shoulders.

'So, Alberto got you here on time?'

She nodded, noticing him observing her choice of clothes from the wide selection on offer, and worried that the approving warmth in his eyes made her feel good, not to mention *aware*.

For a brief childish moment she was tempted to counteract the feeling by explaining that she hadn't been seeking his approval when she selected the vivid mustard wrap-over pencil skirt with the bright blue cabbage roses on it and the classic navy silk shirt.

'He told you, didn't he? Alberto told you.'

His brows lifted. 'I have not as yet spoken to Alberto.'

'I asked him to take me to the Merlin. I wanted to say goodbye to Grandpa. Don't worry, he refused.'

'Excellent. I won't have to sack him.'

Her eyes widened, the horror morphing into annoyance when she read the gleam in his eyes. 'Very amusing, and actually I think the media storm, or at least the worst of it, might have passed.'

Soren, clean-shaven and looking utterly relaxed, eased his broad shoulders into the leather of the seat.

'You think?' His jacket was gone and his long brown fingers picked at the knot of the discreet grey silk tie that lay pale against the dark blue of his shirt, the deep colour intensifying the shocking cerulean shade of his eyes.

Breaking the hypnotic contact, she pushed her glossy freshly washed hair behind her ears and nodded, explaining.

'I would have worn dark glasses and no one would recognise me in these clothes.'

'Shades… Oh, why didn't you say? That would have made all the difference. Were you thinking of a hoodie too…?'

Her lips twisted in annoyance. 'I don't think this is funny,' she retorted haughtily.

'We are on the same page there. Neither do I.'

Looking at her suddenly made him angry— she worried about her grandfather, who was worthless. The woman didn't seem to realise that a conscience was excess baggage.

Soren thought he had eradicated his years ago— he'd had the best teacher—yet every time he looked at her his conscience ached like a muscle memory.

He focused instead on his anger. There was plenty to go around: he was angry at himself and angry at her and the real focus of his fury had been placed out of his reach.

'Perhaps we should concentrate on the things we have in common.'

She frowned, not trusting this sudden bridge-building. 'What are they?' It had to be a *very* short list.

'A library that needs sorting,' he said, his thoughts a million miles clear of his professional delivery.

So long as it was his *thought*s there was no problem, so long as he never lost sight of the in-escapable fact that she was his enemy's grand-daughter, and as such off limits, this could work.

Of course, the situation was not helped by knowing this attraction was mutual. He could have done without the insight—a beautiful woman wanting you was a big turn-on.

'Do you have any doubts you're up to the job?'

She blinked, thrown by another of his light-ning changes of mood. 'Is this an interview?' Or a change of mind? Her professional pride in-jured, her chin went up. 'I'm very good at what I do,' she said, adopting what she hoped was a coolly professional expression—the cool wasn't so hard, as he'd made her feel so angry. 'And I'm actually excited about the challenge.'

His glance was drawn to the soft outline of her mouth. 'Good to know. So it is agreed, going forward, we focus on what we have in common, not what…sets us apart.'

She nodded and sat there looking at him, try-ing not to think about the differences between them: his hardness and her softness, his olive complexion and her pale skin, his… God, the more she tried not to think, the more she *was* thinking. Each thought leading her deeper into a sensual maze, imagining not just the texture of his skin, but how it would feel to touch, how it would feel against her own. His mouth…

'Am I boring you, Anna?'

She gave a shocked little gasp as his voice jolted her from her fantasies. A wave of shamed guilt washed her pale skin rose and she laughed far too loudly to hide her embarrassment.

'Sorry, I didn't catch…?'

'I was saying that nine to five is not really an option. The heat at the moment makes the middle of the day hard to work in. You have no problem with flexible hours?'

'None at all,' she responded, feeling happier about things she felt totally confident about. Workwise she had no false modesty. She knew her worth: she was good and she planned to be better.

'I am looking forward to enjoying our perfectly professional working relationship. How's the foot?' His eyes slid down her bare legs to her ankles. Her feet were covered by a pair of flat ballet slippers. The leather was butter soft and so comfortable underneath the light padding, she had forgotten about it.

She fought the twin urges to tuck her feet out of sight and stare at his wide sensual mouth.

She lost both battles. 'Much better, thank you. These shoes are really comfortable. About that… they sent far too many clothes.'

'I will speak to someone about that.'

'You have to let me know how much I owe you.'

'I'll let you know.' He paused, his chin resting on his steepled fingers. 'Is there something you want to tell me?'

It was worrying he could read her so well. 'I'm still getting calls from journalists,' she admitted.

'I'd be surprised if you weren't. My advice is to block the numbers and switch your phone off if you need to.'

'I had one caller who said he followed us to your mother's apartment building. He knew that you spent the night…' She paused, waiting tensely for his response, relieved when he appeared thoughtful but relaxed as he digested the information.

'What did you say to him?'

'Nothing. I mean, *literally* nothing.'

He smiled. 'You did the right thing. You have his number?'

She nodded and handed him her phone. 'It's the eleven thirty-one call.'

He nodded and transferred the relevant information to his own phone before returning hers. 'Don't worry, he thinks he has a lever.' The hauteur in his face, the ice in his eyes made Anna *almost* feel sorry for the journalist.

'And he doesn't?'

'No, he doesn't.'

'If he calls again?'

'Say you do not discuss your personal life with the press.'

'Personal…but won't he think that you…me… I…?'

'He already does, but people do not print anything about me unless they are very sure of their facts.' He shrugged. 'I'm not known for sitting back and, erm, *taking* it.'

'My visit to Grandpa would have been a mistake, wouldn't it?'

Her expression prodded his sympathy into life. 'Who knows?'

'I said goodbye via video call.'

'That went well…?' he said, studying her face.

'No… Yes… That is, one of the trustees answered initially and I could hear him in the background and then Grandpa looked directly into the camera. I'm not sure if he could see me but he…he just…*snarled* at me to keep my mouth shut or I'd regret it… He looked…'

The protective urge to comfort her, even if that comfort was based on a false premise, was too strong for him to combat. 'Do not overthink it. He is not himself most of the time.'

Her smile still held an edge of the seeds of suspicion he had seen in her green eyes, the suspicion he knew that she would not admit even to herself.

'That's true. Other times, though, he is sharp as a tack. He doesn't always know who I am when we play chess but he wins…he genuinely wins.'

'And when you return, I imagine he will not know you were away.'

She nodded. 'I suppose you're right. The staff have said they will let me know if there is any… change in his condition. So how long is that likely to be, do you think, before the job is over?'

'Shall we just call this an open-ended arrangement? Unless you want something less irregular…a contract with—'

'No, that works for me.' That was probably what all the women said to Soren before he broke their hearts… Luckily this was a purely business arrangement.

One of the flight attendants passed and Soren spoke to her in Italian. 'I'm having a coffee. Would you like anything?'

'I usually have a brandy before take-off to steady my nerves… It's sort of a…thing for me…' The effect of hanging in the air in a large lump of metal that any enterprising bird could down if it felt so inclined did not even make the same page as flying with this man. 'Is it too late now, do you think?'

His lips quivered. 'I thought you didn't like brandy.'

'I like landing a lot less and it doesn't really matter what it is.'

'Fair enough, anaesthesia it is.' He turned to the attendant and said something rapid in Italian.

'So, you were brought up speaking three languages,' she said enviously.

'Everyone in Iceland speaks English. I learnt Italian later on—'

'Your mother didn't…sorry, I'm being… Thank you.' She smiled in gratitude as the attendant brought her drink.

'My grandfather had some sort of dynastic marriage arranged for my mother, but she met my father. When they married my grandfather disowned her. She never spoke Italian to me or spoke of the Vitale family.'

His matter-of-fact delivery was almost as shocking to Anna as the facts themselves.

'So, my grandfather was your father's friend, not just colleague?'

The muscles around his jaw quivered as he fought to maintain his languid pose, resisting the urge to reveal the truth, reveal that the old man she revered was actually a callous, manipulative, lying bastard.

'He knew all the family.'

'I really don't understand why he never spoke of his time in Iceland.'

He tilted his head in a neutral acknowledgment; he didn't trust himself with any other response.

'There is so much I didn't know, and now it's too late.'

He felt his anger drain away as the tightening in his chest made him wonder if the cabin hadn't suddenly depressurised. The husky note in her voice touched him in a place he hadn't known existed. If she had sobbed and looked sorry for herself he would have been fine, instead—instead he was experiencing one of the emotional responses that his grandfather had taught him to equate with weakness.

'I was young when your grandfather was in my family's life, a teenager. Everyone over twenty seemed old to me, and I was pretty much only interested in my own life and ambitions. Before his death, I barely had a conversation with my father. I didn't have a clue what was going on with him.' He had often wondered if, had he not been so self-obsessed, things might have been different. The lingering guilt was something he had never shared and now...to her... His eyes went to her face, which was predictably softening with empathy.

How the hell this woman survived in the real world when she emoted all over the place was a mystery to him, almost as much of a mystery as why he was opening up to her. The knowledge brought a dark frown to his austerely handsome face.

She watched as his dark lashes came down, filtering out the expression she had imagined she'd glimpsed in his cerulean eyes, something close to shock.

'That doesn't make you an unusual teenager.' He might have been an average teenager, but he was not an average man, and it was not just that he was so incredibly off-the-scale good-looking, it was the currents below the surface of calm, his complexity reflected in the way his eyes could change from ice-cold frigidity to volcanic smouldering emotion.

Anna wasn't sure which end of the spectrum was easier to deal with. The entire unpredictability factor made him exhausting to be around… and then there was the added complication that she knew what it felt like to be kissed by him.

Soren watched her take a massive gulp of brandy and choke a little as it hit the back of her throat, and he thought about tangling his fingers in her hair, dragging her face up to his and kissing her.

One of the more sensible pieces of advice his grandfather had given him was *Never sleep with the help,* and he ought to know. It was a badly kept secret that a housemaid Biagio had impregnated had a pension for life and a nice house in Palermo.

The only thing she'd had to do was sign away her unborn child's rights to the Vitale estate. The baby had been stillborn, but to his grandfather's dismay the contract his legal team had written was airtight.

'Have you told any friends where you're headed?' By this point he felt quite philosophical about the answer.

'No,' she said, relaxing as the brandy—or it might have been whisky; it seemed to her they both tasted similar—ironed out the kinks in her spine. She was actually feeling much more mellow. 'I told Sara and Penny that I have a live-in job, not where. They wouldn't talk to journalists anyway.' She ignored his doubtful look and gave her head a sharp positive shake.

She totally trusted her friends. She knew Penny from university, and she and Sara went back to primary school when Sara, a writer these days, had honed her early skills at fiction using the stories Anna told about her mother with some interesting additions of her own.

'Boyfriend?' He threw the question in casually.

Anna, who wasn't looking at him, shook her head. 'Not for a while.' Her brow puckered as she tried to remember the disastrous double date that had to have been a good six months ago now. She liked the safety of double dates. 'Tim, no, *Tom* dumped me. Oh, it's fine,' she added cheerfully. 'He wasn't really my type. Penny has this theory that I only date men I don't really *like* because I don't mind being dumped by them. I think *one* date doesn't really count as *dating*...' She stopped and looked from his face to the glass in her hand. She put the glass down carefully, no longer looking at him at all. 'Can I have some of that water?' she said, nodding at the jug that stood on the table between them.

The ice chinked against the glass as he filled it for her.

'Relax.' He delivered a tight smile, assuming that when she said dumping she was actually the one doing it; the likelihood of a man dumping Anna seemed far-fetched to him. 'I'm not judging. Well, actually, I'm in no position to judge.'

Her sex life was not his business.

Yet you feel such a keen interest in it, mocked the voice in his head.

His hooded gaze drifted over her face, sliding to the cushiony softness of her mouth. He was consumed by a primal urge to part those lips and plunge into the soft sweetness, make her forget every man who had ever tasted her before.

Disconcerted by his unblinking regard, Anna looked at him blankly, thoughts zipping through her head and never quite connecting. She took a deep gulp of ice water and things slotted into place: for *date* he had heard one-night stands.

She opened her mouth and then closed it again. If this had happened with any other man she would have burst out laughing, but she seemed to have had a sense-of-humour bypass.

The irony was, of course, delicious, but he was never going to be in a position to appreciate it, and it was infinitely less embarrassing if he carried on believing she had an impressive back catalogue of lovers whose names she had forgotten, when the truth, the increasingly *embarrassing* truth, was that she was a virgin.

Not a lifestyle choice, just circumstances, caution and a low sex drive and possibly there was a grain of truth in Sara's theory—her friend had a library of self-help books and an encyclopaedic knowledge of them.

Her favourite quote for Anna was: *You have to believe you deserve to be loved.*

Sara *meant* well, but there were times when Anna dreamed of donating her friend's library to a charity shop. Though sometimes she thought there might be something in her friend's more recent theory, which was Anna wouldn't commit because she was afraid of being rejected—her mum leaving her had made her afraid to care enough to have someone walk away.

For Anna it was much simpler: she didn't see the point in sex if it had no meaning for her. Sure, she was curious, but she had a suspicion, like most things that were given a big build-up, it was probably going to be a let-down when it eventually happened.

Her eyes settled on Soren's hands, his long brown tapering fingers—maybe not so disappointing if the first time was with someone who knew his way around—

'I'm going to sit up front with the pilot, a friend… And you couldn't be in safer hands—he's ex-navy.'

She gave a nervy jump and felt the shamed

colour score her cheeks as he got to his feet. Incapable of responding, she just nodded.

It wasn't until he had vanished that she realised she hadn't asked the practical things like what happened when they landed.

CHAPTER EIGHT

ANNA GAVE A sigh of relief as her first ballet slipper hit the tarmac. She didn't go overboard with the relaxation—this was not the end of anything, it was the beginning of a step into the unknown—but before she could get worried about the unknown the heat hit her.

By the time she was ushered into the terminal building her shirt was sticking to her back, but the air conditioning inside was marvellous. The crew member who had escorted her handed her over to an airport official, who progressed her through the formalities in painless moments.

She had refused the offer of refreshments when the suited figures of what she assumed was Soren's VIP welcome committee surrounding the man himself melted away before he reached her. 'Sorry, I had some things to do. You were looked after?'

'Very well, thank you, and there's no need to be sorry. I didn't expect you to come and hold my hand for landing,' she said spikily, thinking, *It would have been a nice gesture, though, considering you knew I was petrified.*

Catching the disgruntled direction of her thoughts, she performed a self-correcting U-turn, reminding herself that she was here as an employee, not a guest. She would have to put some appropriate barriers in place if this was going to work, though the unusual way that this situation had come about made it harder than it would have been otherwise.

'The luggage has been unloaded.'

He dragged a hand through his hair. His jacket and tie were back in place, but the lightly hair-roughened section of brown wrist banded by a wafer-thin expensive watch exerted a stomach-tightening fascination on Anna.

He lowered his arm and she turned away, killing dead her theory that the exhausting electrical atmosphere on the plane might vanish or at least lessen once she had escaped the confined space.

It hadn't.

So live with it, Anna. The only other option was to make a total fool of herself. Even had there been any possibility that he would look at someone like her...though she had noticed that she forgot in his company that she looked like a coat hanger. He didn't look at her as if she were a coat hanger, he looked at her like... She felt the hot shudder low down deep inside and shocked herself back to the present.

She was standing here in a public place having a hot fantasy about who she—

'I'd like to miss the traffic.'

'What? Yes, of course, sorry…flying is so tiring.' She gave a little yawn.

'Well, we could stay overnight here in Palermo, if you like, travel in the morning. We have a house here. The staff—'

'No, that's very…considerate, but I'm fine.'

'Good. I'd planned on getting there before dark.'

'You're driving?'

'You have a problem with that?'

'No, of course, I just thought you had a driver.'

'Alberto has gone on ahead.'

Alberto would reach the palazzo several hours ahead of them, refreshed after a helicopter transfer, which had been Soren's own planned mode of travelling. But seeing how she dealt, or didn't, with flying, he could not imagine that Anna would have coped any better with a helicopter transfer that many would consider breathtaking.

'He drives, certainly, but he's not *my* driver. He multitasks, but he is a security expert.' Security was so much part of Soren's life that he took it for granted, and he forgot sometimes that his life was different from others'. Seeing Anna's eyes widen reminded him that his normal was not normal.

'I like to keep things low-key and, relatively speaking, discreet.' Unlike his grandfather, who travelled with a small personal army, in Soren's opinion more to draw attention than avoid it. 'I also enjoy driving.'

'I hate it. It took me four times to pass my test.'

'Did it not occur to you that someone was sending you a message?'

'I happen,' she retorted with dignity, 'to be a very competent driver. You miss so much when you're behind the wheel and I got full marks in my theory test.'

'Well, that's a clincher. Also, you'll be pleased that this is a very scenic island. Not everyone likes our roads but there are plenty of things for you to see while I drive… Did I mention what a lovely thing it is to drive in silence…?'

She directed a narrow-eyed glare up at his too handsome face and saw the lazy glint of humour shining in his eyes. Finding herself wanting to respond to the gleam, she fought off a smile and hitched her bag on her shoulder.

'Lead the way.'

She'd just said *'Lead the way'* to a man, probably for the first time in her adult life… She knew some women were drawn to men who liked to lead. She was not one of them.

Soren was already striding off, making no allowances for the difference in their leg length.

There was a lot of traffic to negotiate so, despite her determination to keep up a steady flow of chatter just to annoy him, Anna was silent as he negotiated the maze of streets that she assumed were shortcuts.

A few miles after leaving the fascinating architectural mix that was the city, they reached the countryside and she made her first tentative comment. She really didn't want to distract him from the tortuous, steeply rising road they were now negotiating.

'Is Sicily all mountains?'

He flashed her a sideways grin. 'You are not the first person to observe this, and, yes, pretty much mountains and trees, but we have some good beaches, some historical gems and one pretty spectacular volcano. You might,' he teased, 'have heard of it.'

'So I understand.' She closed her eyes as they hit a blind bend.

'I thought you liked the scenery?'

She opened her eyes and directed a resentful look at his perfect profile. 'I also like to live.'

'Relax.'

In truth she was almost glad of the hairpin

bends—at least they provided a distraction from the company. 'How far is—?'

'Just over two hours to the nearest town on the coast. We're inland, in the mountains. Try and get some rest and stop braking.'

'I'm not,' she began, then looked at her foot that was flooring a non-existent brake.

'You have quite excellent reflexes.'

She clamped her lips. 'I suppose you think you're amusing,' she said, lifting her floored foot and realising at the same moment that the road had become a lot less white knuckle. They had reached a flat, fertile plain, with the glitter of azure water ebbing against it, white flecks just visible against the purpling evening sky.

'It's breathtaking.'

'Yes.'

She knew he was not looking at the view, and her sensitive stomach flipped as she looked away quickly.

'I'd feel happier if you looked at the road occasionally and kept both hands on the wheel.' Being enclosed in the same space as Soren felt like a damned hormonal war of attrition.

'You sound nervous… I have driven this route once or twice, you know.'

Anna's heart was in gymnastic mode again as she framed a tight nervous smile aimed somewhere over his shoulder.

'This time of night the mosquitos are hell. Do you mind rolling up your window?'

'Like the Highlands. I bagged a Munro and a billion bites last year.'

'You climb?'

'I hike…gentle hills with well-marked trails.'

'So where do you take your risks…or don't you…?'

They were climbing again, the views either side now cut off by trees. 'I don't see the fun in jumping without a parachute.' She took advantage of his focus on the road ahead to study his face in profile. The angle emphasised the sybaritic slant of his cheekbones. It was easy to see him as an adrenaline junkie. 'And while we're on the subject, do you mind slowing down?'

He flashed her a white grin that made her think of the wolf. 'A man has to remind himself he is alive sometimes.'

Despite the grin and the contention, he did slow a little, but it soon became obvious this was not because of her plea but was because they were approaching a massive set of ornate wrought-iron gates, which swung open as they approached. Presumably their presence had been observed by the strategically placed cameras Anna noted.

'Yes, Big Brother is watching,' Soren said drily.

As the four-wheel drive crunched on the gravel

the gates closed behind them with a clanging finality. In the fading light the road cut into the tall pine trees that stretched out as far as she could see, looking like a dark river lit by regularly spaced illuminated bollards along the winding length.

'Light at the end of the tunnel.' He brought the car to a halt and turned the engine off even though they were several hundred yards away from the forecourt.

'Oh, my!' Anna had reasoned that to boast a library of any size the palazzo was not going to be a farmhouse but the sheer scale was a shock.

'Baroque, neoclassical and Sicilian rococo,' he listed, anticipating her reaction. 'The place took so long to build the fashions kept changing.'

'It's just so vast! And the colour…?'

'Pompeiian red. It makes an impression, hence the white pillars, all a bit…phallic.'

'I think *that* might be in the eye of the beholder.'

His lips quivered. 'As for the size, back in the day the entire extended family would have lived here. Now…well, I am the family.'

Until he had children, she thought, her heart sinking a little as she pictured him with his arms around an adoring tall, beautiful blonde, a gaggle of assorted gorgeous children around them.

'I remember the first time I saw it.'

She shook her head and banished the blonde. 'I forget you were not brought up here.' His blue eyes were the only thing that marked him out as not being totally Latin. How old were you when you…?'

'I was seventeen.'

Her heart ached for him. He'd only been a boy when his family had been hit by tragedy. 'And you'd never met your grandfather?'

He shook his head.

'It's sad it happened that way, but at least your family were reconciled.'

He gave a strange laugh. '*Reconciled?* I suppose that is one word for it. I came to ask for a place for my mother to stay…he set the dogs on me!'

Anna's eyes widened. 'He didn't know who you were?'

'Of course, he knew who I was. Biagio was testing me. He just wanted to see if I'd come back. He said I wouldn't be worth keeping if it was that easy to get rid of me.'

'That's terrible!' she gasped. 'You came back?'

'I had no other option. I was in no position to take care of my mother, we were broke, therefore no choice, and no grown-ups to come and rescue us, and she was… She is fragile and my father's death and scandal, it all affected her badly.'

'Scandal?'

He nodded. 'My father's partner emptied the pension fund and absconded, leaving my father to carry the can.'

'That's why you're helping me—because your father was falsely accused too!'

'It has taken me some time, but I am about to clear his name.'

'That's marvellous. Your mother must be so proud.'

Soren suspected that at the moment she would not be at all proud of him. 'My mother does not do hate… She is into forgiveness. Whereas I *do* do hate. I hated this place with a… I hated it and Biagio.'

'And now?'

She watched him staring at the magnificent building. He was very easy to watch; even his frown was beautiful.

'More of a love-hate thing these days. There came a point, I don't know when, that I found I was happy to be returning. Now I spend more time here than is strictly necessary. People make a place and some good people live and work here, and Biagio has removed himself, which is a plus.'

'So your grandfather is proud of the estate?'

'He has never spent much time here. For him it is a status symbol, no more. The only thing my grandfather loves is money, prestige and power.'

'He sounds terrible!' she gasped, then, when he looked at her, made a self-conscious apology.

'He is what he is…' he observed phlegmatically. 'Thanks to him I have learnt a lot, and most families are dysfunctional.'

Anna thought about her mother and nodded, feeling unexpectedly in accord with him on the subject.

'Actually, my mother rejected me.' She blinked. She had never said that out loud before, never lowered her defences enough to let anyone see the old hurt.

Perhaps, she mused, there was something in the air in this magical place besides the smell of cypress and wild thyme.

She saw his expression and panic slid through her. 'Sorry, too much sharing,' she said, sounding nervous and not quite meeting his eyes, not wanting him to know how vulnerable she felt.

'Probably better than a kid who grows up thinking the only thing they have going for them is a pretty face.'

She looked at him, startled. She had never thought of it that way before.

'Sometimes it's the way you look at things. My grandfather's methods may have been tough, but I learnt the business from the ground up. I never ask anyone to do anything I have not done myself. I have him to thank for that.'

'Where does your grandfather live now?' she said, feeling pleased she was not going to meet the man, who sounded like a total monster to her.

'Whichever marina the beautiful people are occupying—he has taken up residence on his superyacht. He calls it his retirement.'

'And your mother, will she be here?'

'She has a cottage in the grounds. She *might* be here for the ball.'

'Ball?'

'There is the charity ball every year, at the end of the olive harvest, mid-October.'

'So late?' She was surprised.

'It's still twenty-three degrees here then, and the olives are still on the trees. Historically it was a tradition for all the local families to come together—the farms brought their harvest to the palazzo to be milled and the profit was split fifty-fifty. The ball was a celebration of the harvest, a community thing.'

'And now?' She turned away from the illuminated building.

Cynicism crept into his face. 'Oh, now it is wall-to-wall designer, famous faces. It's become a PR event, a marketing opportunity.' His expressive mouth conveyed the depth of his cynicism. 'You'll see for yourself.'

'I'm staff.' And October was a long way off. He dragged his eyes off her face, her skin washed to a silver glow by the moon, and directed his stare at the ancient building. 'Oh, we might let you out of your attic if you're good,' he said, thinking he would very much like to see Anna *bad*.

'Oh, Grandpa would love this…or he would have,' she tacked on sadly.

Her words killed the intimacy and brought reality crashing back. This was Tor's granddaughter, which put her out of reach. While he was rebuilding the walls that he'd lowered, beside him Anna gazed raptly and oblivious at the palazzo.

He started up the engine.

He felt her questioning look but didn't react. Pulling up on the forecourt a few moments later, kicking up gravel as he hit the brakes, he was out of the car before she had unfastened her seat belt and opening the door for her.

She looked confused; he knew he'd see hurt in her eyes if he looked, so he didn't. 'I've still got work to do,' he said shortly. 'It's late so I'll get Domenica to show you to your room. You all right having your supper there?'

Confused by his sudden change of attitude, she followed him up the flight of steps and through the porticoed entrance. Around them she could hear the night creatures, the rustle and cries in the darkness. It was a lonely sound.

They stepped into an overwhelming space lit by a massive chandelier, and she blinked. Faces stared back from the ancestral portraits that lined the walls. The fine stucco panels on the ceiling were decorated with pastoral scenes; the detail, even from this distance, seemed remarkably accomplished.

'Here is Domenica now.'

On cue a woman had silently materialised, wearing a pale silk blouse and conservatively plain pencil skirt; her dark hair was streaked with silver, but her face was unlined. She was very attractive.

'I hope you both had a good journey.'

Soren gave a grunt that could have meant anything, or he might have been clearing his throat. Her confusion tipped into anger.

Was this because he'd let her see that there was a chink in his armour? Was he regretting allowing her to glimpse his vulnerabilities? Or maybe she was the fool seeing a wounded hero, when all he was was a top-of-the-food-chain male animal who used women.

'This is Domenica, who is a great deal more than a housekeeper.'

Now, there was a choice of words to incite speculation, and of course it did, though Anna struggled to hide her thought processes behind a smile.

'Our journey was…long,' Soren said, thinking, *Too long*.

He had only intended to give Anna the basic facts about the palazzo; instead he had found himself opening up in a way that was utterly alien to him. It made him uncomfortable to think about the things he had said to her, inviting her and her small feet to wander around in his head.

The decision to spare her the helicopter transfer had come back to bite him big time… The orally focused thought inevitably drew his eyes to her soft mouth.

The thought of loosening the tight seam of her lips took immediate residence in his mind— He cleared his throat and reclaimed his control.

It was past time to kill off the self-indulgent fantasies. He should not need to remind himself that sleeping with the enemy, or any relation to the enemy, even when that relation excited him to a painful degree, was fraught with complications that were too high a price to pay for a few moments…maybe many…of pleasure.

Anna stood back and wondered if their switch to fluid flowing Italian was intended to make her feel excluded, or was she being oversensitive?

Either way, she did.

The conversation went on above her head as Anna allowed her gaze to flutter around the massive space—everything about it was intended to awe, and of course it did. It remained to be seen what the parameters of this woman's role were, but she did seem to have a very easy relationship with Soren, though intimate might have been a suggestion too far.

'Right, I will leave you in capable hands. Tomorrow—well, it might take you a while to get your bearings.'

'I only need to get my bearing of the library. That's what I'm here for,' she said, pleased to see a flash of something close to surprise in his eyes. He wanted things on a business footing and that, she told herself, was fine by her.

She didn't look back as she mounted the staircase behind the older woman, even though his footsteps had stopped and she could feel the imaginary imprint of his eyes between her shoulder blades like a laser-guided gun sight.

The woman gave a running commentary on the history of the building as they walked along seemingly endless corridors. Anna's brain retained a few descriptions, such as Sicilian Baroque, but for the most part the information slid over her head.

A few of the many doors they passed were open; she would have lingered at some, but the woman's pace was as relentless as her delivery of detail.

Anna was relieved when she finally came to a halt.

The attic that Soren had taunted her with was a suite of rooms that were beyond luxurious, and, despite the ancient fabric, the plumbing was five-star state-of-the-art decadence.

She salivated at the idea of testing out the massive marble tub or, for that matter, the shower that was twice the size of her bathroom at home.

When the subject of supper was introduced, Anna shook her head and patted the crewel-work cover of the four-poster they were standing beside. The bed had been turned back and she recognised one of her new nightdresses arranged artistically on the silk cover.

She resisted the temptation to say *What? No chocolate mint on the pillow?* and smiled. 'Actually, I'm not hungry. The tea—' she nodded to the table beside the fireplace filled with an urn of fragrant flowers, where a tea tray with a snowy cloth was set '—will do me just fine.'

The woman gave a gracious nod. 'Well, if you are sure. There are cold drinks in the fridge, but should you change your mind or want anything at all, just dial zero.' She indicated the old-fashioned phone set on a bedside table.

After a short solo exploration Anna found all her personal items along with her new wardrobe, which must have travelled ahead, laid out neatly in the cavernous drawers and wardrobes of the separate dressing area.

She finally kicked off her shoes and, with one of the silver-backed brushes from the dressing table in her hand, wandered into the football-pitch-sized bathroom—a slight exaggeration, but not much!

Taking the lids off some of the row of crystal glass-topped bottles, she inhaled the various fragrances before selecting one. Sitting on the edge of the tub, she switched on both taps and poured some of the oil into the gushing water. It immediately foamed and filled the space with the exotic fragrance.

She let her clothes drop where she stood and stepped into the scented water, willing her mind to go blank as the warm water did its magic on the various tense knots in her body.

She might even have fallen asleep, if the water hadn't cooled and a low distant rumble hadn't made her lift her head.

Wrapping a sarong around her and towelling her wet hair, she padded back into the bedroom in time to see a flash of light at the stone mullioned window; the accompanying rumble came some time after.

The storm was a long way off.

She pulled on the neatly arranged slip that lay

on the bed—having someone pick out her night-dress for her was a first—and climbed into the bed feeling like the princess in one of her favourite childhood fairy tales. She had once taken a pea from her dinner plate hoping to be able to feel it, but she had failed the royal test miserably.

CHAPTER NINE

SHE HADN'T EXPECTED to sleep but, under acres of goose down and silk, exhaustion claimed her almost immediately. Her awakening was as abrupt as her sleep was deep and dreamless. Sitting bolt upright in bed in the pitch black for several seconds, she did not even know her name, let alone where she was, and then the total blackout was briefly broken by a flash of white light that seeped around the heavy drapes outlining the two windows on the opposite wall.

A second later the crash came, no longer a distant rumble; it sounded as though it was directly overhead. Reaching out in the darkness, she fumbled for the lamp, a few more fumbles and she found the cord switch—nothing happened.

She took a deep breath and waited for the angry rumble to pass. Anna was not terrified of storms, but they were not her favourite thing.

She used the next flash of lightning to locate her phone and switched on the torch.

Her relief was tinged by caution when she saw that the charge was low. She slid aside the covers; a quick tour of the room's light switches confirmed her initial suspicion that there was a power outage.

She picked up the old-fashioned internal phone and noted that it did indeed rely on the power supply and the charge on her phone showed her only light source was about to run out.

The idea of cowering under the covers for the rest of the night while what sounded like Armageddon raged outside her window did not hold much appeal.

Switching off her torch to conserve what power she had, Anna was about to lie down when she remembered the burnt-down candle beside the bath that had made her wonder who before her had used the bathroom, and had a couple shared the massive bath.

She made it to the bathroom just as the power on her phone faded out.

'Do not panic, Anna.'

Her words were drowned out by an extra-loud thunder crash. Arms outstretched, she visualised the room in the dark, managing to find the cool marble edge of the bath.

She considered one bruised shin after a misstep was a price well worth the prize when she located the candle and the silver matchbox beside it.

The one match inside made her heart drop a little but, with an expression of fierce concentration on her face, she took a deep breath and struck the match. Still holding her breath, she applied it to the candle wick.

A moment later the small flame caught, and the room was gently illuminated. Her initial triumph was short-lived when she saw how little of the candle remained. Her light supply was still limited so it looked as if sleep was her only option. The depressing thought triggered a light-bulb moment—which seemed pretty appropriate in the circumstances.

She was sure that she remembered the row of stone niches just before they reached the door to her suite, each one filled with an ornate candelabra complete with candles.

It had been really close and she was sure it would be easy to locate, she just had to literally follow her nose.

It became apparent very soon that her confidence was misplaced, the following-her-nose thing had not worked out so well and, as the candle she was carrying was burning low, the sensible, actually the *only* course of action left open to her was to retrace her steps.

As she reached a second junction that she had not previously noticed she didn't even bother debating which one to take; it didn't matter. She was totally lost in this damned maze of a castle wearing nothing but her nightdress—however this situation ended, it was not going to be ego-enhancing and it was going to be in the dark.

If she found her way to her bedroom, it would be sheer luck, and hers, and the candle, seemed to be running out.

She was debating what would happen if she just screamed out for help when the corridor was lit by a lightning flash that came through an open door to her left. As the thunder rumbled she stepped towards it, pushing the heavy metal-banded door, which swung in silently to reveal a room that was so massive her flickering candle barely penetrated the blackness. As she was about to step out there was another lightning flash that shone in through a row of high windows that almost reached the black-and-white-checked floor of a room with a dizzyingly high vaulted ceiling.

Before the lights faded she saw the echoing space was totally empty apart from a grand piano in one corner and, of more significance, the candles sitting on the stone sills along one wall—not one or two, but dozens.

She stumbled a little in her haste as she

crossed the room and, by some sort of miracle and with the help of her tiny guiding flame, which was getting fainter by the second, found them at the first attempt. Her hand shaking, she held her breath as she lit the first one, which revealed a jar of long tapers, so, putting down her guttering candle, she picked one up and began to light the others, leaving a trail of flickering flames in her wake as she moved down the room.

After the next lightning flash, the room was not as dark and she stepped back in awe, her head falling back to view the awesome splendour of the frescoes painted on the intricate barrelled ceiling.

Anna did a slow full three-sixty spin. She was standing in the middle of a ballroom straight from a fairy tale. Windows down one wall, a massive fireplace on the opposite one. The rows of chandeliers suspended from the intricate ceiling caught the candlelight and revealed the steps she had avoided bumping into at the far end that led to the raised dais that housed the grand piano. There was enough room for a full orchestra to join it.

Utterly enchanted, she forgot that she was lost, forgot that she was barefoot and dressed in a nightdress, and she climbed up on the dais and lifted the lid of the piano, pressing a key… Hearing the sound bounce back at her, she really wished she could play, but despite her lack of skill she could hear the music in her head.

The gym was at basement level and the music playing in his ears had drowned out everything else as he pounded his way up a virtual hill, pushing his body to the physical limit and then beyond, working towards some sort of relief from the hunger that was gnawing at him. It was not complicated, it was sex, hormones—his need to reassure himself of the fact was annoying.

He had decided that the simplest way to cope with the disruptive influence on his peace of mind that was Anna Randall was to remove himself from the situation. Less a retreat and more a strategic withdrawal.

Immersed in his private physical combat seeking the level of exhaustion that would give him some relief, he didn't reach relief but at least a workable explanation for the situation. He did not deal with celibacy well and Anna Randall had arrived right in the middle of a dry spell. His first inkling that there was a storm raging anywhere but in his head was when the lights went out.

Cursing at the interruption, he removed his ear plugs and waited, with the sweat cooling on his overheated body, for the emergency generator to kick in. It didn't.

Locating his phone and then a towel, he headed for the shower, catching his breath as he stepped into the unheated stream of water, which, while not his choice, was probably not such a bad thing. It took the edge off the frustration that had robbed him of sleep, but it didn't make the face, the voice and the body that had robbed him of peace of mind vanish.

Retrieving his shorts but leaving the sweat-stained vest on the floor, he hooked the towel over his shoulders to catch the drips from his saturated hair and gave the lights one more try before he walked past the glass-fronted lift and made his way up to the ground floor using the spiral flights of stone steps, their surface worn by the generations of feet that had used them before him.

At the top of the stairs he gestured to the dogs who were silently shadowing him and after throwing him a canine look of reproach—they had been hoping to sleep on his bed—they peeled away, heading towards the kitchens and their beds.

The storm was still raging; he could feel the static of electricity in the heavy air. Even though the rain had not begun to fall yet, he accepted it would be suicidal to venture out to check out the backup generator, which was housed—rather impractically, he had always thought—in a building that was hidden by a bank of tall cypresses. One had fallen last year and just missed the roof.

He wondered as he made his way to the back staircase that led to his private apartments what other damage might have been sustained to the buildings. Having been born in a land that was exposed more than most to raw nature, he felt a certain affinity with the extremes of nature the mountains here offered.

He was halfway along the corridor when above the rain, which had just begun to fall and was lashing against the windows, he heard the tinkling sound of a piano chord.

The incongruous sound froze him in his tracks.

He knew where the only piano in the place was located, but why anyone would be in the ballroom at this time of night eluded him.

Perhaps, he mused, one of the ghosts he had heard so much about but never seen was out and about. It was not white apparitions rattling their chains that had troubled Soren's sleep. He had hoped his own ghosts would be laid to rest after he had exposed Tor; he should have known that life was never that clear-cut.

There was no music coming from the ballroom, but light was leaking into the darkness through the half-open doors.

Soren slid his phone into the pocket of his

shorts and stepped inside his trainers, making no sound on the floor.

The sight that met him stopped him in his tracks; his chest lifted as he breathed in sharply. The light he had seen came from the candles all along one wall...a remnant of a photo shoot his grandfather had given permission for the previous month.

To Soren's annoyance and the staff's great inconvenience the place had been invaded by a famous photographer he'd thought was long dead, an incredible number of people who it seemed were required for a fashion shoot, and the models themselves, beautiful women who posed in very little clothes that cost an impossible amount of money. The candles were meant to lend atmosphere but had apparently not been moody enough.

They had been extinguished and left.

They were burning now and so was he.

The flames flared and the vaulted ceiling reflected back the light, leaving the checked pattern of the floor flickering on the walls.

He barely registered these details. He had hardly breathed since he had walked into the room, not once his eyes had focused on the supple figure who, arms crossed over her chest like some sort of sacrifice, was swirling around the floor in circular patterns. Her eyes were closed, her slim, vulnerable neck extended, her hair a silk cloud down her back as she moved to the music in her head.

Wind found its way through the invisible cracks in the ancient stone window frames, making the candles flame and dance and causing the silk slip that ended mid-calf to flutter, drawing even tighter against her body and clinging like a second skin to the lovely line of her legs and the tight roundness of her behind. She suddenly spread her arms wide, causing one thin strap to slip down the smooth curve of her shoulder, the action revealing her high pert breasts, the nipples pushing through the thin fabric.

Fire slid in a steady pumping stream through his body. Something moved in his chest—it felt like fingers closing around his beating heart. He couldn't breathe.

If he took another step, if he crossed that line, Soren knew there would be no going back. She was who she was, that could never change, and she didn't know who he was.

He *knew* everything inside him told him that if he took that fatal step there would be consequences to pay, but from the first moment he had set eyes on her he had wanted her…wanted her in a way that had nothing to do with logic or sanity. He ached for her in his bones.

It was as if she had set fire to some primal instinct in him, Soren thought as he watched her twirl. He had never seen anything as beautiful and desirable as the dancing figure. Her beauty touched him and the desire overwhelmed him absolutely, wiping his mind clear of any thought other than possession. There was no space left for reasoned thought; its absence left just instinct and blind, relentless hunger.

Enemy, lover, the words had no meaning; nothing had meaning but the need pounding through him.

He might well regret this tomorrow, but he could not think beyond the here and now, and the need to possess her had his heart pumping a steady stream of logic-defying lust through his body.

'May I have this dance?'

Anna, who had heard nothing but the sound of the music in her head, gasped and fell off the balls of her feet with a bump.

'Soren!' She had just been imagining she was in his arms and now he was here, unless she'd gone mad, which was a distinct possibility. The clash of dream with reality in the form of flesh and blood... She lost the thread of her thoughts as her eyes did a head-to-toe-and-back-again survey.

In a suit he could stop traffic. It turned out that

not wearing a suit, in fact wearing very little, he could stop the world on its axis!

The earth-stopping little consisted of a pair of shorts that hung on his narrow hips and revealed every inch of his muscle-ridged flat belly. He had the sort of lean, muscular, not-an-ounce-of-spare-flesh body that a professional swimmer spent a lifetime trying to achieve.

She could see his wide shoulders cleaving through the water and his long muscular legs… Actually, she could see them tangled in her own, which only added to the reality-meets-fantasy vertigo she was suffering.

'I was looking for a candle,' she heard herself say.

'You found a few,' he said, his eyes leaving her face but only for a split second. 'Dance?'

Was he making fun of her?

'There's no music.'

'I can hear it,' he replied, taking her waist and the situation into his own capable hands.

His hand on her waist brought home belatedly her state of undress, which was equal to his… She panicked, then stopped as, holding her eyes, he caught hold of her right hand, placed it against his chest and stepped into her.

Before she could protest—she liked to think she would have—he began to move. At that moment even the theoretical possibility of resistance vanished.

He was tall, she wasn't, this shouldn't have worked but it did—the differences were part of the formula that made it work. He was hard, she wasn't; even with her sharp angles and lack of curves she had never felt softer and more female in her life, as they continued to circle the floor, both hearing the same song.

As if in a dream Anna felt she was floating… it might even be an actual dream…

Jolted free of the lovely place she had inhabited by an extra-loud rumble of window-rattling thunder, she gasped and instinctively burrowed closer as his arms moved to encircle her. When she tried to pull away, he held her firm, one hand now splayed across the curve of her taut behind. The other moved to the back of her head and a finger at the angle of her jaw tilted her face up to his.

He looked so beautiful so predatory that she ached.

'You're a very good dancer,' she said, making herself think about all the women he'd practised with—and she wasn't thinking dancing—just to cool down the fire inside her. Masochistic, yes, and it didn't even work. The fire carried on burning… He was just so beautiful.

One hand was trapped between them, the

other she raised and laid on his shoulder, before allowing her fingers to slide down, feeling the quiver of surface muscles as she spread her fingers down his back.

He swore… They were no longer dancing, they were standing stock-still in the middle of the room, both barely breathing, staring at each other.

The thickness in the atmosphere had nothing to do with climatic conditions.

Bad idea, Soren!

He tried to listen to the voice yelling in his head, he made a genuine effort, but passion, lust, her passion-glazed eyes and parted lips drowned out the voice of reason.

He held her eyes and jerked her in hard, smiling a skin-prickling predatory smile when she whimpered as his erection ground into her belly.

'I have a serious problem with your mouth.'

The electric touch of his finger on her lips made her quiver. 'It's too big, I know,' she pushed out breathily.

'It's perfect. It just makes me so hungry…and you make me…' The rest of his words were lost inside her mouth as his tongue slid between the seal of her lips, deepening the combative clash of tongues and teeth.

Outside the thunder crashed and a pane of glass cracked, causing the nearest candles to gutter and die in plumes of dark smoke. Neither of the figures engrossed in each other noticed; the touches and sighs, the deep, drowning, hungry kisses grew wilder and fiercer until Soren, breathing hard, put her from him.

'My room,' he said thickly, before he kissed her hard.

Anna wound her arms vine-like around him, revelling in the hard, hot heat of his body. Her face level with his bare chest, she pressed openmouthed kisses against his golden skin, tasting the salt, loving the texture.

He dug his fingers into her hair, yanking her back to look into her face; a moment later he was sweeping her off her feet and into his arms.

Anna wound her hands around his neck as he carried her from the candlelit room. The dark closed in but he seemed to know where he was going; he *definitely* knew what he was doing.

Occasional lightning flashes illuminated their route, throwing out eerie monochrome flickering images on the walls as they progressed up a flight of spiral stairs.

A door kicked open hit the wall and made something in the room fall and smash; the noise barely penetrated her sex-soaked brain. They fell together onto a bed and as he shifted himself off her for a moment, she breathed for what felt like the first time in minutes as she sank into the mattress and gazed up at the man kneeling over her, who looked like the living embodiment of the storm that raged outside, primal and wickedly exciting.

Her brain was mush; she *ached* for him. Reacting to the throb of need between her legs, she reached up her hands, fastening them to his hips, and she pulled him down, arching to meet his body, hungry for the contact.

The eyes looking up at him were green pools of confusion and need that Soren could readily identify with. She was vibrating with tremors that shook her entire body. He had never known a woman who was this responsive; he'd known the passion was there but the intensity of it still surprised and excited him. She was a temptation that he could not resist.

The sliver of silk she wore was the only thing between his bare chest and her skin, and then it wasn't... Anna wasn't even aware of him peeling it off, until she experienced the first breath-catching skin-to-skin contact.

She gasped at the heat of his skin, and then as he pulled back to look at her she felt the first stab of self-awareness and awkwardness as they lay side by side facing one another.

He was so perfect and she... Thinking of the women she had seen pictured with him, women that were everything she was not, she lifted an arm to cover herself. 'I'm—'

A finger pressed to her parted lips, he cut off her words. 'You have the most perfect, sensual body, elegant...sleek, exquisite. I want to see you, *cara*.' His throaty whisper against her neck made her shiver and drop her hand.

He took the action to be an invitation and his hand dropped from her flushed face to her small, smooth breasts; the peaks hardened and pinched tight under his scrutiny and his husky, fervent, 'Perfect.'

Anna felt excited and empowered and unbearably aroused as his blue eyes moved hungrily over her body, the scrutiny accompanied by a low growl, half appreciation, half pain.

The carnal intent on his face made her pull back, but not because she didn't like it, not that it didn't excite her.

'No, Soren, I have to tell you this...'

Something in her voice, the urgency, penetrated the fog of lust in his head. Breathing hard, he rolled away from her and lay on his back, one arm curved above his head, his flat belly sucked in as his chest heaved. The eyes that stared back at him were wary, filled with need, glittering like twin emeralds. Looking at her, he felt something beyond lust, something he denied a name, something it would be safer to detour around, but it didn't go away.

'Look, I'm not sure if this makes a difference to you but the one-night-stand thing…'

'I'm not interested in your sexual history.' He was only interested in making her forget it and every other man she had slept with. He did not doubt for a second his ability to do so.

'That's the point. I don't have any.'

He'd been staring up at the ceiling but at this he turned his head her way, the flush along his cheekbones making them look like razors. All his features were more sharply defined. The deep febrile glitter in his darkened eyes made her shiver low in her belly and wish she hadn't told him and risked this not going any further.

If he rejected her now, she'd die.

'What are you trying to say?'

'I am saying I'm…well, I suppose…a virgin.'

CHAPTER TEN

HE LOOKED AT her as though she were talking a foreign language. The muscles along his jaw quivered. 'Is that a joke?'

'A person has to have a first time.'

Not with me, they don't, he thought, but somehow the words never made it to his lips, because he was looking at her mouth and it was hard to speak when he did. He just wanted to taste her.

'And I was a late developer,' she added, glancing down and giving a little grimace.

It seemed to her that his anger came from nowhere.

'Do not do that!' he growled, taking her face between his hands and throwing one heavy hairroughened thigh across her hips.

'What? I…' Her wide green eyes reflected her bewilderment.

'*Believe* you're beautiful.' He took her hand and placed it against her own breast. 'Just feel how beautiful you are.' His fallen-angel grin gleamed white as he stared down into her shocked face. 'Say it!'

'I'm beautiful,' she whispered and felt every inch of her skin prickle with heat. 'Oh, God!' she groaned as she reclaimed her hand and held it above her head, hiding her eyes.

But he took her left hand instead. 'That's better. I want to see you.' He kissed his way up the curve of her neck.

'It's all right, you know,' she whispered against his cheek, before licking a wet trail across the sensual curve of his upper lip and kissing the corner of his mouth. All the while she tasted him her hands were moving in circular sweeping motions over the hard muscles of his shoulders and back. 'I just want to live in the moment. I want this, you, now, Soren.'

Her throaty plea broke whatever bonds remained, desire overrode everything, sanity vaporised in the heat that flared white hot between them as he rolled her under him and began to kiss her, the air around them shimmering with the heat the entwined pair were producing.

She gasped and moaned as he touched her everywhere, wakening nerve pathways, pleasure pathways she had never known existed. She clutched at him, revelling at his hardness and strength, responding to instinct as she arched into him, not wanting to be closer, wanting to be part of him.

He levered himself away for a moment, but it was only to divest himself of his shorts. Her insides liquefied as she watched him through the shades of her lashes, her cheeks flushed with passion, her small breasts rising and falling in tune to her shallow, fast inspirations.

Her scrutiny seemed to arouse him even further, if that were possible. She had to satisfy her carnal curiosity. Rolling a little to one side, she reached out, and, tongue caught between her teeth, she ran her fingers down the silky hard length of him, before her hand tightened around him, drawing a deep fractured groan from his lips.

She gave a small whimper of protest as he took her hand.

'Not now, I can't...' His face was a primal mask of need as he pinned both her wrists above her head with one big hand and, arching over her, kissed his way down her quivering body.

Her thighs parted to aid his carnal exploration of her most intimate core, the intensity of the sensations sweeping through her so intense that the pleasure bordered pain.

As he touched the aching area where her pain was centred she pushed against him in the grip of a hunger beyond anything she had ever imagined.

She grabbed his head and pulled him down, not sure what she was babbling against his neck, but he seemed to understand her incoherent pleas as he ran a soothing hand down her face before kissing her, a deep, drowning, painfully slow kiss that relaxed the taut muscles in her body.

On some level she was aware of him reaching for a condom, but then he settled between her legs and her awareness contracted, focused on his dark beautiful face, until nothing else existed.

'Put your legs around me, *cara*.'

She responded to the growled instruction without taking her eyes off him. The stripped-back raw expression on his face was utterly riveting. He bent in, his lips teasing and taunting her mouth, dipping in and out of the honeyed wet interior with his tongue.

Her ankles tightened around his waist to increase the tortured pressure at the juncture of her legs, growing slick as the pressure increased.

Her body arched as he entered her, her eyes squeezing tight shut as, with a series of sharp pants, her sweat-slick body adjusted to accept him. All her being was focused inwards on each new sensation as pleasure pathways awoke, as she moved with him as he touched places deep and then deeper inside her, part of her.

Then, just at the point when she really thought

she was losing her mind in the delirium of pleasure, he whispered in her ear, urging her to let go, to trust him.

She did.

She didn't fall back to earth, she floated back…

It was the sun shining directly in her face that woke Anna. She lifted a hand to shield her eyes and stretched languidly. She grimaced—she felt stiff—and her eyes flew wide. Lying there on her back, staring at the ceiling, she reached out and patted the bed either side. One side carried a slight dint, cold as if whoever had made it was long gone, the other revealed a nightdress.

Clutching the nightdress to her chest, she sat up and looked around the room she had not seen in the light. It was empty. The night's events slid through her head, from the dancing by candlelight to the making love for the second time, just as intense but slower and even more mind-blowing than the first time.

She'd been wrong: the reality had turned out to be not a let-down at all; the reality had turned out to be incredible! She looked around the room again and a flicker of uncertainty found its way to her face.

She was no expert on morning-after etiquette,

but waking up alone did not feel like the perfect way to start the day after the night before.

Pushing aside the rumpled bed covers, she pulled the discarded nightdress over her head and, wriggling her way into it, got out of the bed.

She looked around, not sure what to do, apart from the necessary, which required a bathroom. The first door she opened was a large walk-in wardrobe with pretty monochrome contents; the next was the bathroom. It was just as luxurious as her own but with a much bigger shower and less choice on the perfume and potions front.

She emerged five minutes later feeling more comfortable. She'd tamed her tangled hair with a silver-backed brush and given her hands and face a perfunctory wash but had resisted the temptation of the shower, and was glad she had when the door opened and Soren appeared.

Her heart skipped a beat as she stood there leeching composure, then she noticed he was not alone.

Her eyes flew from his face to the two powerful-looking dogs, pale gold in colour. They had dark masked faces, almond-shaped intelligent eyes; their muscular, powerful bodies seemed to quiver with energy.

'This is Ragnar and Rok.'

'Clever,' she said, sending him a shy smile. He

was wearing a shirt open at the neck, the sleeves rolled up and jeans that were dusty at the knees.

'Boys, this is Anna.'

'Are they safe?'

His eyes glimmered, the high-voltage smile appearing and causing the expected damage to her nervous system. 'Not a word that I would use, but they are extremely well behaved, and you are totally safe, always supposing they don't think you are attacking me.'

'I'll keep that in mind,' she said, moving towards where they both sat like sentinels. 'What breed are they?' she asked, holding out her hand.

'Malinois… Belgian Shepherds, intelligent and smart. They get bored easily and need a lot of stimulation.'

A bit like their master, she thought, wondering how long it would be before Soren was bored with her…maybe he already was?

Tickling one of the animals behind his ear, she pushed the question away, telling herself that *she* might be the one who got bored first.

You keep telling yourself that, Anna, mocked the voice in her head.

'Good boys,' she said, smiling as they each licked her hand after sniffing her.

Watching with a half-smile, Soren laid a tea tray on a small table. He clicked his fingers and the dogs padded away and lay down, heads on paws beside the bed.

'You were sleeping. I didn't want to disturb you. I had an early morning call. The standby generator, the roof was taken down by a fallen tree, some emergency repairs were required.' He relayed the situation in a verbal shorthand that gave her the relevant details quickly. 'It's up and running now. Apparently the mains electricity won't be online until later.' He held her eyes. 'That was quite a storm last night.'

'I won't forget it.'

The way his eyes darkened made her sensitive stomach muscles quiver. He dragged a hand through his dark hair. 'I need a shower. Help yourself to tea or coffee. I won't be long.'

'I need a shower too,' she called after him.

He stopped, framed in the doorway, his eyes gleaming wickedly. 'What are you waiting for, then? An invitation?'

She released the tense little breath she'd been holding and, feeling bold and channelling her inner sensual siren, she strode past the dogs and into the bathroom after him.

He was already unbuttoning the shirt. Unable to take her eyes off him, she watched him, the knot of anticipation in the pit of her stomach tightening painfully.

Soren lifted his head and looked at her. 'You

like to watch?' he purred, dark challenge in his eyes.

'I like watching you,' she whispered as the shirt hit the floor. His hands were on the belt at his narrow waist now as he walked towards her, stopping within a couple of inches of her unzipped, and let the jeans slide down his legs. Stepping out of them, he stood there in just his boxers, which did nothing to hide the extremity of his arousal.

She felt the pulse of need in the slick heat between her legs and felt her self-control slipping like sand grains through her fingers. She didn't try to catch them, welcoming the liberation of giving up control.

She shivered as his eyes locked on hers. She hardly recognised the instincts that had taken control of her, but amid the glorious confusion in her head she knew she'd be safe with Soren, in a very dangerous way.

As he kicked himself free of the boxers she couldn't stop her eyes dropping. Her inner temperature jumped several mind-numbing degrees as a raw longing slid through her shaking body...

God, yes, she was shaking...

God, he was so beautiful.

'Now you, I think.' Leaning over her, making her more conscious than ever of his physical dominance, he took the hem of her nightdress and peeled it over her head in one practised motion.

'Pretty,' he said, throwing it over his shoulder. 'But this…oh, yes…this is very much more… more everything.'

He leaned against a pad on the wall and the shower kicked in; taking her hand, he pulled her with him inside. They stood there face to face, the pulses of water hitting them from all sides drenching them in seconds. None were as powerful as the sensations ripping her apart inside or as sharp as the spiralling excitement that held her in a vice-like grip.

'Here, let me.'

She saw the bar of soap in his hands, watched him work it to a lather and cover one breast, his fingers gliding over her wet skin as he stroked and massaged, leaning in, one hand braced on the glass wall above her head, so that she kept receiving a tantalising nudge of his erection. She tried to push into him but he held her off.

Then he turned her around. Anna, in a delirium of pleasure, laid her hands flat on the glass wall to stop herself falling as he began to run his shapely hands down her body, massaging and stroking down the length of her back and then her bottom, and—

She gave a broken cry as his hand slid between her legs parting the sensitive folds of flesh. Just when she thought she would die from the pleasure of it he turned her around to face him.

Their eyes connected, his navy with passion, and the moment stretched until it snapped and he caught her by the waist, lifting her up as he slid hard into her. Anna wrapped her legs around his waist and let him take her to some place inside herself, some place deep and hot she'd never even dreamt existed.

As she stepped out of the shower her legs felt so weak he had to support her. Picking up one of a stack of towels, he tenderly dried her off.

'I didn't do anything for you,' she whispered.

His laugh was deep and warm. 'You do everything for me, *cara*, but, if it makes you feel any better, next time it's your turn.'

'So there will be a next time?'

Her smile faded as she watched an odd expression drift across his face, robbing his eyes of warmth.

'Perhaps we should…slow things down a bit?'

Her smile froze as the hand she had lifted to his face fell away. 'Slow…?' she repeated. The word still didn't make sense.

'Get to know one another.'

Anger, hurt and self-disgust rushed into her head, making it spin.

He had set out to use her and she had let him. Last night for him had been just sex and that was all he wanted, and it turned out the sex wasn't even interesting enough by his high standards to want more. She was just a boring little virgin.

'Anna, this is not—'

'Personal... Oh, I know.' She took a deep breath, pinned on a brilliant smile as her deep hidden fears rose up to mock her: she was not a lovable person. Only they weren't irrational fears after all. It was true.

'This is not about you, it's me...' he said between clenched teeth. 'There are things—'

'Wow, that is *so* original,' she drawled with mock admiration as she cinched the towel so tight across her breast that it hurt. 'You know, I would admire you more if you were simply straight with me... No, it's fine,' she tacked on, mirroring his step forward with two hasty ones back. If he touched her she would forget her pride, what there was of it, and make a fool of herself. 'And you're right—let's keep this professional. You're paying my wages. We shouldn't be sleeping together.' She could come out of this with her pride intact, if not her heart.

'This has nothing to do with work.' He hated seeing her hurt, hated being responsible for it, because he had been too impatient to wait.

Wait for what, Soren? It's not as if you wanted

*a deep and meaningful relationship—you
wanted sex, you got it.*

She arched a brow. 'No…?'

What could he say to her—that he'd set out
to use her? That he'd let his own need outweigh
every consideration, her inexperience? He'd been
so blinded by lust that he'd almost forgotten to
use protection and she was so inexperienced
she'd not even registered the fact. At least he
didn't have that on his conscience—if he hadn't
looked after her, he would never have forgiven
himself.

He wasn't going to tell her any of that, or
that he'd believed the worst of her. That in itself
seemed ludicrous at this point.

The only lies had been his and… *Dio*, he really had laid the foundations of this mess, and
as for truth setting him free?

Not on this occasion.

Last night had been the moment for truth or
restraint and he had taken the third path, and
now the truth would cause more damage than
silence… If he told her now he would be the
monster, not Henry.

Why should he care what she thought?

But he did!

The irony of this situation was not lost on
Soren. For the first time in his life he was thinking of something *beyond* casual sex; he was in

virgin territory, quite literally, and he was pushing the woman he wanted more from away.

How much more he didn't know—he was the one who felt like a virgin.

It was a situation of his own making; he had known there would be consequences, and there were. Consequences to sleeping with her without telling her the truth. She had slept with the person she thought he was; the reality was something different. Last night he just hadn't been able to resist her; the way she made him feel bypassed all logic.

Her beautiful face was closed off and hard. 'Right, I'm late for work. I don't want to make the boss mad. Late on my first day not a good look.'

The dogs, alert to the human emotion in the air, began to whimper.

Soren held up a hand and they both slid down onto their haunches, ears pricked but silent, their almond-shaped eyes moving from one human to the other as they lay there panting.

'Anna!'

She flung off his hand. 'Which way is my damned room?' She sniffed.

He moved in front of the door and stood there like a sentinel. 'Last night…you were the best sex I have ever had in my life!' he pushed out in a driven voice.

She stopped dead, her anger peeling away to leave just the hurt exposed, which from Soren's point of view was worse.

'Why would you even say that?'

'Because it's true and I don't want you to walk out that door. You are *exactly* what you seem to be… I am not. There are things you don't know about me yet, things that might make you feel differently.'

'Then tell me.' What? she wondered. What could be so bad?

'It's complicated and I'm not sure you're ready to hear what I need to say, and until you are… can we get to know one another? Do the normal things that people do…?'

'A date, you mean?' She turned over this choice of words in her head. Best sex, while flattering, was not exactly an avowal of love, but you couldn't fall in love in days; she had never believed that. She believed love was something that grew out of respect and shared values, laughter?

His brows lifted and an odd laugh emerged from his lips. 'I hadn't thought of that, but why not? Sure, a date.'

'*Best sex?* Really?' She thrust out one hip to a provocative angle and moistened her lips. 'Sorry,' she said in response to his deep groan of pain. 'But I've been going slow all my life and I have a lot of catching up to do.'

'Sometimes, Anna, the only way to move forward is to go backwards.' Even to him that sounded like running away, and would that be such a bad thing?

Maybe it was the honourable thing, because he knew, even if she didn't at this point, that Anna was in danger of falling in love with him. With the realisation came the understanding that, even if he hadn't known it, a woman's love was something he had been avoiding all his life.

Backwards...? Anna could not think of any situation where what he said was true, but she let it pass. He had trusted her with his secret, or at least allowed her to know it existed, and that had to mean something, didn't it?

No one falls in love in days, Anna. She repeated the words in her head until the flurry of panic passed.

'Well, don't ask me to forget last night happened because I couldn't if I wanted to and I don't!'

'You don't regret it?'

'Of course not.' She thought about asking him if he did but she wasn't sure she'd like the answer.

CHAPTER ELEVEN

So he'd lasted an entire day.

He had fought the fevered mind-numbing hunger and won. Of course, he had removed himself from temptation's way, actually put several hundred miles between himself and the source of his ultimate desire, but all was fair in lust and... He inhaled sharply as that source came into view.

It was definitely too soon to declare victory!

Thanks to the incline of the undulating path she was walking down he knew Anna wouldn't be able to see him for another few moments, which meant that Soren did not have to filter his stare.

His hungry blue eyes burned with a flame as hot as the fire inside him as he watched the slim figure approach. She moved with a natural grace that made him think of a ballet dancer; her hair was loose the way he liked, the sunlight picking out the darker titian threads in the waves that fell on her bare shoulders.

The simple square-necked dress she was wearing was sleeveless and cinched in at the waist by a narrow silver belt before falling into a bias-cut skirt, the fluid fabric suggesting the outline of her shapely thighs as she moved.

'Hello.' She tried not to eat him up with her eyes, but she was pretty sure she was not succeeding. Her room was littered with outfits discarded during her hunt for something that fell into Soren's interpretation of *casual*, which had been his one-word response to her texted question.

His casual, it turned out, was an open-necked pale blue shirt, sleeves rolled up to the elbow, and a pair of black jeans that made it hard for her to lift her eyes and her mind from the hot place they had sunk to.

She watched him pull out designer shades and thought that was an excellent idea as she rummaged for a pair of her own and hid behind the oversized dark lenses, aware as she did so of him uncoiling his long lean frame from the gleaming sports car.

'You look lovely.'

Glow was an acceptable response to the compliment, but the furnace that lit inside her was not.

She wafted a hand across her face and murmured an explanatory, 'So hot.' Before tacking

on an unwise, fervent-sounding, 'So do you—
look lovely, I mean,' as she slid into the low-
slung car, grateful that she'd chosen to wear flats.
She'd have definitely fallen off her heels.

The car purred silently into life. She was glad
the roof was down—the breeze and the scent of
pine diluted his unique male fragrance that made
her awareness of him ten times worse.

'Where are we headed?'

'The coast, to a little place that not many tour-
ists have discovered yet. Do you like seafood?'

'I do.' If the conversations stayed this simple,
she could cope.

'Then it was a good choice.'

'I can make up time by working this evening,
unless this is a working lunch?' Sometimes you
had to ask if you wanted to know.

Their eyes met briefly before he refocused on
the road ahead. 'It isn't.'

'So it's a…?'

His lips twitched. 'It's a date… You are very
persistent, *cara*, you know that?'

'It's lunch time and your text was…' Brief
and to the point, signed off with his initial. It
had not involved any avowals of love—*in your
dreams, Anna*—or even lust… She would have
settled for *I'm missing you* or even *I'm looking
forward to seeing you.*

If it hadn't been for the distractions offered by the library, he would have invaded her thoughts to the exclusion of everything else—even in the library she had found herself wanting to share a new and exciting discovery with him.

'You can have dates at lunchtime.' The timing was not an accident or even convenient, but candlelight and Anna might prove too potent a temptation for his willpower.

A man needed to know his own limitations and since Anna had appeared in his life Soren had been redrawing his. Possibly payback for being smug about his iron self-control?

'You want the roof up?' he asked, aware in the periphery of his vision of her struggle with her glossy hair while he wanted to feel it against his skin as she sat astride...

'No, this is lovely. Sicily is very beautiful... oh!' She bounced a little in her seat, hand still clamped to her hair. 'I can see the sea!'

'Next you'll be asking me are we nearly there... Not long now. Another fifteen minutes.'

The small village consisted of a long straggle of pink-sugar-coloured houses along the shore of what appeared to be a working fishing harbour. Driving past nets strung along the sand, Soren pulled up beside a few other cars parked alongside a whitewashed building built into the stone wall of the harbour.

'This is a beautiful spot.'

'I hoped you'd like it.'

As they were escorted by a suited figure through the rustically decorated interior where most tables were occupied, she knew all eyes were on them, or at least on Soren, but she pretended not to notice. Soren didn't need to pretend; he was, she realised, genuinely oblivious.

Seated at the gingham-clothed table on the wooden deck constructed over the water, Anna looked around from under the shade of a parasol that fluttered gently in the breeze.

'Oh, they don't seem very busy,' she remarked, surprised at the empty tables and wondering why anyone would choose to eat inside.

'No, they don't,' Soren, who had booked out the entire outdoor seating area, agreed. 'Oops!' he added as her elbow caught a glass.

The butterfly touch of his fingers on her wrist brought their eyes, no longer protected by tinted glass, on a collision course.

Anna heard him swear. She couldn't have said anything to de-escalate the tension even if her throat hadn't already closed. Her brain might have frozen, but her senses had not!

A waiter appeared, oblivious to the atmosphere, though his expression did alter slightly as he met Soren's eyes.

Soren began to translate the menu and, though normally she would have enjoyed asking questions and making her own choice, she was seized by the sudden strong urge that this just be over with; it was a bad idea.

It was agony!

'Choose for me,' she said, thinking, *Words I never thought I'd hear myself say.*

He dragged his eyes away from the sensual promise of her plump lips. 'That doesn't sound like you.'

She looked straight at him. 'I don't feel like me.'

In his mind he saw himself swiping the crockery from the table and taking her right there and then as he laid down the menu, gave the order and said, 'They do the best prawns here.'

The food was delicious, and the wine, which Soren, as designated driver, didn't touch, helped take a few of the kinks from her spine and the panic out of her eyes. It also inevitably made her quite talkative.

She looked at her empty pudding bowl and up at him, realisation settling and bringing a worried frown to her forehead. 'I've probably been boring you, but the library really is…amazing.'

Boring, no, driving him insane, yes, the way her beautiful little face lit up with animation when she spoke of the books she loved... He could have watched that for ever and as for her voice... *For ever?*

When did that happen?

He dragged a hand across his jaw as his blue stare skidded away from hers. 'Do you want coffee or shall we...?'

His abruptness and his obvious desire to get the hell out made her wonder...*was their first date going to be their last?*

Of course, if the stars had been out and the drive had been moonlit on their way back, the sexual electricity zigzagging back and forth in the car would have had an inevitable ending. But there were no stars or moon and Soren had turned his mobile on speaker and their return journey involved a three-way conversation in a foreign language to which she was a miserable listener-in.

If he had wanted to kill the mood, he could not have arranged things better.

Anna got the call from the Merlin just as they got back.

She glanced at Soren.

'It's the Merlin. Grandpa had some blood tests yesterday. I have to take it.'

He watched as she walked up the path, the receiver pressed to her ear. He could see the worried stiffness in her spine and found himself wanting to lighten the burden she was carrying.

What happened to simply wanting to take her to bed?

Anna spent the evening in the library, heading there like a homing pigeon seeking the solace of the books. It was several hours before she became so engrossed she stopped waiting for Soren to come and invite her to share dinner with him.

The next day she decided not to wait. If he wanted her, he would have to do the looking; she was not hanging around for him. Feeling rebellious and miserable, she took a coffee and croissant into the library and had barely sipped the scalding liquid when Soren appeared.

She fought to retain the coolness she had decided to treat him with and lost. After all, he hadn't actually done anything to justify her resentment except not touch her.

Remembering how his touch had made her feel things, had sent her deep into herself to a place she hadn't known existed, caused her to choke on her hot coffee.

'You weren't at breakfast.'

'You noticed.' She closed her eyes and winced, opening them and offering a twisted smile and—'Sorry.'

'I was wondering about your grandfather's blood tests…?'

She was touched by his concern; her forced smile became genuine. 'They were OK, actually, and the clinic have taken on extra security, which makes me feel easier, but I worry.'

'Why?' Her worries were his… The admission hovered somewhere unacknowledged in the back of his mind.

'Well, security doesn't come cheap, but they haven't even suggested Grandpa leave and I thought they might,' she admitted.

'Why would they? He's fetching them a lot of publicity and there's no such thing as bad publicity.'

'They have been very understanding.'

They had been very astute; he had funded the security, but they had held out for an addition to their physiotherapy team.

'I just can't understand who would be low enough to do this to Grandpa, what sort of low life…'

Soren cleared his throat. 'You're very close.'

'Grandpa was always there. If it wasn't for him social services would have put me in care, and he never made it seem like it was a bother, though I'm sure it must have been. He came to all my parents' evenings, flying in specially from business sometimes. I can't imagine what my life would be without him.'

'And now you are there for him. You might,' he began softly, 'need to be prepared to hear some bad things about him.'

'Oh, I've heard what they are saying…and I can't wait for the day when they are going to have to apologise.'

'You are so convinced your grandfather is innocent?'

She stiffened and glared at him, her tension levels in the red zone in seconds. 'Of course he is innocent!'

Her defensive stance made him wonder if maybe she wasn't having doubts of her own, doubts she was not ready to own—yet.

He watched as she got out a pair of white gloves. She made him think of a bright light in the middle of the dusty book-lined room.

'Looks as if you have made a lot of progress in my absence.' It looked exactly the same as when he'd last been here to Soren, but his housekeeper, deeply impressed by Anna's work ethic, had assured him that she had spent every waking moment in here during his day's absence.

'This is much more than…' she sighed, turning a full three-sixty as she took in the crammed shelves '…than I ever imagined.'

He watched her move around the room with

every appearance of having forgotten his existence, reverently opening pages of volumes thrown casually on the table and pulling others that caught her eye on a shelf, exclaiming as she made each fresh discovery.

Finally she paused and faced him.

'You do realise how rare some of these are? I have never seen so many first editions,' she added excitedly. 'There are volumes here that were assumed lost...'

'So, valuable, then?'

'There is a small fortune...no, actually, a very large one on these shelves and the condition of some...' She shook her head reproachfully. 'It's disgraceful.'

'Sorry,' he said meekly, drawing a reluctant grin from her.

'I got a bit carried away but, in all seriousness, this is a very special collection. You might want to have someone more experienced than me.'

'I wouldn't change your experience for the world.'

The message in his eyes sent a throb through her body, and her interest in the rare books declined.

She brought her lashes down in a silky veil. 'That's good to know,' she said softly.

'I'll leave you to get reacquainted with your books, but if you feel like cooling down before dinner…the outdoor pool…? I'll be there around five.' Leaving the offer open, he left.

At five thirty-one—Anna didn't want to appear too eager—she arrived at the pool fed by a mountain spring, built into natural rock and boasting breathtaking views of the mountains, which some mornings, Soren had told her, were reflected in the still green surface.

Anna was eager, and she was determined; she had had enough. She could not last another day, another hour, another minute like this! Her jaw tightened. Him holding her at arm's length was a challenge she had decided to accept.

The surface was not still as she approached, though the economic strokes as Soren powered his way up and down barely made a ripple.

She stood at the side, watching this display of power and grace as he cleaved through the water.

She sensed the moment he registered her presence.

He paused and began to tread water. Pushing his wet hair back from his face, he grinned through the drips.

'You coming in?'

'How do you know I can swim?'

If he didn't touch her she'd die—or she'd kill him for doing this to her.

'Can you?'

'Not as well as you. Is it cold?'

'Fed by a mountain spring is the clue.'

Anna took a deep breath and, very aware that he was watching her, she loosened the tie around the silk kaftan that had come in one of her packages along with two swimsuits and a bikini. She had finally opted for the plain black swimsuit. Cut high on the leg revealing what felt now like acres of bottom, it had a deceptively modest V-neckline at the front but the back was cut almost to her waist. The stark simplicity was relieved by a thin chain belt.

She draped the kaftan across one of the chairs set around a table, walked to the edge of the pool and performed a creditable dive.

The cold hit her heated skin and made her gasp. She kicked hard and with a sinuous little wriggle came up for air a few feet away from Soren.

'You're a water baby. Race?'

She shook her head. 'I'm not in your class,' she shouted back.

Soren had clearly adjusted his pace because there was no way she could have kept up otherwise as they swam several lengths side by side in silence.

It was Anna who stopped, breathless, and flipped onto her back, arms spread, using the occasional kick to keep herself afloat as her hair hovered around her like fronds of seaweed and she turned her face to the last rays of sun hitting the water. The rest of the pool was already in shade. 'I'm out of condition.'

'You look like a mermaid,' he said, coming up beside her. 'And your eyes are the same green as the water.'

She gave a lazy kick and flipped over onto her stomach. 'Race you back!' she yelled, already several feet ahead as she struck out.

'You cheated.'

'You won.'

Grinning, he heaved himself in one lithe motion onto the side and, bending down, held out his hand. After a moment she took it and allowed him to haul her out.

She landed lightly but almost overbalanced and fell into him. She stood there and stared at him through her wet eyelashes, sleek and so perfect it made her ache just to look at him. 'Sorry.'

He experienced a bolt of pure blinding lust that literally immobilised him. 'You all right?'

She shook her head. She hadn't come here looking for love, but it had found her. 'I stubbed my toe.'

'You're shivering.'

'I forgot to bring a towel.'

'Share mine,' he offered, bending to pick up his discarded towel from the floor. 'Come sit over there in the sun. You'll soon warm up.'

Wrapped in his towel, she followed him across the paved area to the carved oak chairs with cream cushions set around a table. The parasol was down and the table was in full sunlight.

'I could get some drinks sent down if you like.'

'No, thanks.' She handed back the towel and their fingers touched, not accidentally, on her part at least, and stayed that way...

'No!' she snapped suddenly pulling her hand away. 'I don't want to hold your hand. I want to—' She stopped and bit her lip. When she looked up he was watching her with eyes that had darkened to navy.

'What do you want to do to me, Anna?'

She shook her head, sending a shower of icy droplets around the immediate area. They sizzled and died in seconds on his hot skin as he leaned in close so their faces were touching, his nose against hers.

'So whisper if you can't say it out loud.'

Frantic with longing, Anna closed her eyes and did.

He lifted his head and looked into her eyes. 'There are all kinds of slow.'

Her insides fluttered and grew hot. 'There are?'

'Absolutely.'

She nodded and fell into him with a sigh of

relief as his lips clamped down hard on hers. 'I can't keep my hands off you,' he groaned out. 'You can say whatever you want to me, you know. Would it help if I told you what I want to say to you, what I want to do to you, have you do to me…?'

Frantic with passion from the seductive voice in her ear, she nodded and whispered, 'Please.'

'Someone might come,' she said a while later as she fought her way into her swimsuit.

Soren watched her contortions with a lazy smile. 'No, I swim naked normally, so people keep away. Did I buy that swimsuit?'

'Yes.'

'It was worth every penny.'

'Does no one else use the pool?'

'Most people prefer the indoor heated…my mum swims in the sea usually, but she comes here sometimes. I think she misses the hot springs at home. I'll take you there some time. It's quite an experience.'

She didn't take the offer seriously, but it was a nice thought. Two days—if it hadn't been for the library she might have gone mad, but it had given her time to think, maybe too much time, and she didn't know an awful lot she hadn't before, but she did know that whatever this was… whatever she felt, or didn't, she wanted to extract every last moment of pleasure and build as many memories as she could.

Which probably translated as she was his for the taking… Did he want to take her?

'This must be quite a change from Iceland for her.'

'Mum is Sicilian. It's Dad she misses.'

'Sorry.'

'I found him.'

She dropped down beside him at the table and touched his bare arm. 'You're cold.'

'He took his own life.'

'Oh, Soren…'

'I was mad with him for so long for leaving us. It's not true that it's an easy way out. It's not…easy at all. It's ugly.' Anna listened in horror, afraid to move or say anything in case he stopped.

She watched as the glazed look in his eyes suddenly cleared; he blinked and looked at her as if he was shocked to see her sitting there.

'If you want to talk.'

He looked at her hand on his arm and laughed. 'I have spent the last twelve years trying not to think about it. Talk? That's the last thing I want to do.'

She thought of the pain and memories he had hidden away and her heart ached for the boy he had been and the self-contained man he was now.

She had let down her barriers and allowed him in, but she could not see him ever letting her in.

'Well, if you ever do…you know where I am.'

'So how long will the library keep you here?'

'The library is not a month's work, it is more a lifetime's work, but I'll be here as long as…' She shook her head. 'Although, I have to go home soon. My grandfather's condition is not going to improve. He is very sick. He needs me.'

'You can't go!' He intercepted her startled look and made a corrective tone adjustment. 'Yet. You can't go yet. You've barely started.'

'I'm loving it,' she said, her wistful expression fading as somewhere in the back of her head a voice added, *I'm loving you.* 'But I have to go at some point.'

CHAPTER TWELVE

Soren had decided to walk rather than drive. The track through the forest was only just over a mile and it was clear most of the way.

When he arrived at his mother's cottage she was in the garden, straw hat on her head, watering the herbs she cultivated.

His suggestion he install an irrigation system for her to cut down on labour had been politely refused. There was pleasure in the work, she said. Why would she want to cut it down?

She smiled when she saw him and then as he got closer and she could see his expression her frown appeared.

'What's wrong?'

'Not wrong, right… I found Tor Rasmusson. I didn't want you to find out from someone else.'

She nodded. 'I never doubted you would.' She searched his face. 'It does not appear to have made you very happy…but then revenge rarely does.'

'I cannot forgive and forget as you do. I am not that person.'

'I don't forget,' his mother corrected gently. 'There is more, isn't there? Come sit in the shade and tell me.'

Soren gave his mother a potted version of the story. The only time she looked surprised was when he told her that he had brought Tor's granddaughter here.

He outlined his reasons—well, not all of them.

'I think that was very kind of you, Soren.'

'I am not *kind*.'

'It's not a shameful thing, you know,' she said sadly, 'to care about someone else. You're fond of this woman, aren't you?'

'She is Tor's granddaughter.'

'You are depriving yourself of so much pleasure in life.'

Saving himself from so much pain, he thought, wondering how she could still believe this when losing the man she loved had nearly killed her.

'I am using her.'

'Oh, Soren!'

'It's true. I wanted to see if I could trip her up… I wanted her to be guilty.'

His mother said nothing as Soren stared broodingly into the distance.

'She is his granddaughter. How can I ever forget that?'

'How will you know unless you try?'

Soren stared at his mother. 'And you wouldn't have a problem with that?'

'Life is short, Soren, too short to let a chance of happiness slip away without even trying.'

'What would be the point? When she finds out that I outed Tor, who she thinks is some sort of saint, she will never forgive me.'

'Oh, Soren... I hate to repeat myself, but how will you know until you try?'

For the first time Anna was not eating dinner alone and she had dressed for the occasion: a turquoise chiffon slip dress that swirled when she moved. Her foot had healed enough for her to slip on some heels, and she had pinned her hair into a loose pile on the top of her head before freeing a few tendrils.

The conversation, thanks to the presence of waiting staff, was pretty stilted.

Then finally they were alone.

Soren seemed tense, she assumed something to do with the business that had taken him away.

'I have been thinking about what you said about going home and I want to propose a compromise. You could commute.'

She stared at him. 'Between Sicily and London?'

'I do...'

'That is not practical and you know it. I'll help you find someone to replace me. There are actually a lot of people who are better qualified than I am.'

'It's not your qualifications, it's your…enthusiasm.'

Anna paused with her fork in mid-air, about to put a mouth-watering spicy prawn into her mouth.

He planted his elbows on the table and mirrored her actions. 'I actually would like to be closer to your…enthusiasm.'

Her eyes darkened and danced. 'In that case, shall we take our puddings to my room?' This might not last for long but she was going to extract every single moment of pleasure that she could.

'You want a pudding and me…' He waved a hand across the table. 'After what you just put away.'

'It's my metabolism. I can eat what I like and never put on an ounce. I know, I've tried. Anyway,' she added, getting to her feet and shaking out the napkin that had been lying across her knees, 'I can always take more pudding.'

A lot later that night she realised that she could always take more Soren. Her appetite for him seemed to be utterly insatiable.

'Are you asleep?'

She lifted her head off his warm chest; in the darkness her eyes were luminous. 'Nearly.' She yawned.

'Sorry.' He started stroking her head again. 'Go to sleep.'

She sighed and sat up, the covers sliding to her waist. She marvelled at how unselfconscious she felt, knowing he was looking at her, liking that he was looking at her. The knowledge made her nipples, still tender and aching from his recent ministrations, harden.

'What is it?'

'Nothing…'

He rolled away and she stroked his smooth back, enjoying the way the muscles contracted under her fingertips.

From nowhere, it seemed, he asked, 'Do you remember your father?'

'No, I was a baby when he drowned.'

'So you have no memories of him? How I envy you!' he pushed out in a growl of pain that shocked her.

She pulled herself against his back and laid a hand on his chest. Where his heart had been thudding slow and strong moments before, it was now pumping frantically, seeming to be trying to batter its way out of his chest.

'You must miss him…?'

There was a long silence. 'I remember him...' he said, his mind sliding back to that day. The window he'd come in to latch still banging as the storm outside picked up, the smell of the place, hay—he still couldn't stand the smell of hay. 'I knew he was dead, but I couldn't, I *wouldn't* let myself believe it.'

She bit her lip to stop herself crying out, afraid that if she did or said anything he would close up again like earlier; he would freeze her out the same way he froze the world out.

Her tender heart ached for his pain.

'I tried to wake him up and then I just... I hate that he'd been alone and I didn't want to leave him alone...' She slid her hand into his, interlacing their fingers before she carried his hand to her lips.

'A neighbour came and found me...called the... I hated my father then for what he'd done, for leaving us, and later I found out why and discovered there was someone else who was to blame.'

'I hope that person rots in hell,' she declared fiercely.

'My mother does not believe in revenge—she believes in love.'

Love was feeling another person's pain as if it were your own, it was wanting... Her thoughts froze. This was love; what she was feeling was love. She'd fallen in love with the real man, not the man the world saw, but the man she could feel shaking, the man who had protected her from a sense of honour that he would have denied.

'I should not be dumping my rubbish on you!' he suddenly said, rearing up in the bed, the anger in his voice aimed at himself.

'That's what…friends are for,' she said, glad that in the dark he couldn't see her brushing the tears from her cheeks. She couldn't have love, she'd take what she could get, but her heart was his whether he wanted it or not. She had no choice.

Her heart ached for him.

Her heart ached for herself.

She loved him.

She pretended to be asleep when he slipped from her bed in the early hours.

This morning as they sat across the break-fast table the awkwardness in him was obvious. What was also obvious was that he was regretting revealing the part of himself he had last night.

'Please don't shut me out,' she said quietly.

'I need a therapist. I will visit one. I need a woman in my bed. I will take one.' The brutal words were intended to hurt but he got little pleasure from the pain in her eyes.

'Fine,' she said, thinning her lips to hide the tremor and folding her napkin with careful precision. 'I'll go to work.'

She did but halfway through the morning she took off her white gloves and headed for the door. He was trying to push her away, but she didn't have to let him.

Without really knowing why, she made for the swimming pool, and he was there, eating up length after length with a metronomic precision that she found riveting.

She knew that he was aware of her presence, but he didn't immediately stop; she was prepared to wait.

Finally, when he levered himself out of the pool and stood there, the water streaming off his sleekly muscled, powerful body, the sight of him almost broke her resolve. He really was the most beautiful thing she had ever seen in her life.

'I want to talk to you.'

'We are talking,' he said as he began to scrub at his dark hair with a towel.

'This is business. We need a business setting.'

He stopped rubbing his hair and let the towel hang loose around his neck as he moved forward. She would have mirrored the move only a step backwards would have put her in the water, so instead she stuck out her chin and stood her ground.

'What business?'

'I need… I *want* to go and see my grandpa. According to the clinic, things have cooled down.'

He arched a sardonic brow. 'You are asking my permission?'

Her jaw clenched. He really could be an arrogant bastard when he wanted to be. 'No, I am damn well *not* asking your permission. I am asking if you want me to come back.'

He looked as shocked as she'd ever seen him; his eyes slid from hers in a very telling way. 'It's complicated.'

'It's not that complicated,' she said.

He laughed without humour. 'You have no idea how complicated this is.'

He moved away as if to dive back in and she felt her temper flare. 'You know, Soren, while you're swimming up and down you might like to reflect that you're not the only person who has suffered some trauma. Your dad left you because he was ill—mental illness is as much an illness as any physical ailment. My mum left me because she thought I was boring—that's not such a nice thing for a little girl to know.

'You know, I used to think that she might have stayed if I was prettier. She likes pretty things. I was a major disappointment. I didn't even fill out.' She glanced down at her non-existent bust.

His heart raged at the thought of this callous bitch. 'Your mother is a selfish narcissist!' His eyes flared, sparking blue contempt and fury, his heart aching for the little girl she had been.

'I'm not going to disagree with that analysis, but it took me twenty-four years to reach the same conclusion…

She paused while he swore with an inventive fluidity in several languages.

'Oh, I know it's not in the same league as what happened to you.' Compassion softened her eyes as she continued but the passion had drained away, leaving her feeling pretty damned vulnerable. 'But the point is…' She stopped and drew a deep breath, and realised that actually she had no idea what the point was.

'Well, you can tell me all about your complications in, what shall we say…twenty minutes?' Without waiting for a response, she stalked off, head high.

Anna walked back through the garden. It covered acres and an army of gardeners kept it immaculate. She had explored a fraction of it, and it was now entirely possible she might never get to explore the rest.

Of the areas she had explored there was one that had already drawn her back. She headed that way now because what it lacked in formal planting, classical design or manicured green expanses it made up for in soothing charm.

She had started the familiar circuit when Ragnar and Rok appeared, as they had begun to do. They fell into step at her side even after she had opened her hands to reveal she had no treats.

Maybe it was the canine-greenery combination, but she felt the calm working its magic as she walked through the dappled shadow of the soothing glades where the organic planting blended seamlessly into the encroaching wild countryside it bordered.

She left more composed but still not sure if she really wanted to do this, if she wanted to push things this far, when she knew it might not work out the way she hoped.

It was in this ambivalent frame of mind she arrived at the area of the palazzo that was a home office, but not in the conventional sense. There were several satellite spaces, a conference room, a gym, and Soren's private domain, a large room with an outer office.

There was one person in the outer office, one of the assistants who seemed to operate on a rota basis, working, as far as she understood, between Palermo or Rome and here. She knew this woman's face but not her name.

The woman had no problem identifying her, but then the fact she had divided her time here so far between the library and Soren's bed probably made her stand out.

There were few mistress-slash-librarians around.

She might even be unique.

The woman slung a laptop case over her shoulder. 'My transfer is waiting, he isn't here yet, but go through,' she said, with a wary eye on the dogs, who hadn't waited for an invitation and when Anna entered had already settled themselves on the leather chesterfield.

Anna didn't sit down. She walked down the room, gazing but not seeing any titles in the book-lined walls to distract her.

She had issued what amounted to an ultimatum and she was regretting it. The timing, she decided, was wrong; she should have waited.

For what? For him to realise he's wildly in love with you? The only place that's going to happen is in your dreams.

She shook her head to clear the mocking voices. That they were not going to end up together was pretty much a given, but if anything she said or did helped push Soren in a direction that led to healing the wounds he carried from his past, that could only be a good thing.

The strident ringing of the landline on Soren's desk made her start, then as the ringing stopped and the message machine kicked in Anna began to move automatically towards the door.

Though it would be hard to eavesdrop when the one-sided conversations seemed to be in Italian, she had started to recognise the odd word and phrase.

She was actually at the door when she heard a familiar name, at the same moment the person speaking switched seamlessly to English, the way she had heard Soren do on many occasions.

She recognised the voice, identifying him as the young lawyer she had last seen cycling away. She turned and stood beside the desk, unashamedly listening to the lawyer give a detailed report.

By the time he was finished she was deathly pale and shaking; inside she felt frozen.

When Soren walked into the room, he knew there was something wrong, something badly wrong—he could literally feel the waves of tension rolling off her hunched body.

His intention was to tell her the truth, finally, but the second he walked in he knew that this wasn't the moment.

'What is wrong?' Only one thing he could think of would make her look like that. 'Is it your grandfather?' He had lifted his hands to frame her face when she placed both her own hands on his chest and pushed viciously hard.

'Do not touch me, you bastard!' she growled, putting all the venom and hurt she was feeling into the one word.

'Anna, what…?'

'My grandfather? Yes, it *is* my grandfather. I hate to disappoint you, but he's alive.'

It was at that point he saw the light flashing on the phone on the desk and he closed his eyes.

'I don't know what you heard.'

'I've heard that you planted the lies about my grandpa!' she bellowed incredulously. 'And now you've decided to blame him for your father's suicide, which of course is brilliantly convenient when he can't defend himself.' She looked up at him with an expression of supreme disgust on her face. 'You're twisted, you know that? Not content with punishing an innocent, sick old man, you thought you'd really stick the knife in by—'

'I was trying to protect you.'

'Oh, God, yes, I feel *so* protected.'

He winced at the acrid bitterness in her voice.

'If protected means lied to and used and… Was it your plan all along to make me fall in love with you?'

'I never wanted to hurt you, Anna. I tried to keep my distance, but you are so… I was wrong about you.'

'Oh, God, yes, I'm gorgeous,' she drawled sarcastically. 'And if you were wrong about me, why can't you be wrong about my grandpa?' She lifted a shaking hand to her head. Her choice was brutal—either her grandfather was a monster or the man she loved was.

'This isn't what it looks like...'

Her breaking-glass laugh cut across him. 'And I was *grateful*!' She pressed a hand to her mouth. 'I feel sick...' She swallowed and revived enough to fling out with spitting fury, 'I also feel so stupid, but, you know, some day soon I'll start feeling less stupid, but you... you...you'll always be a total, complete bastard!

The muscles around his jaw quivered but he said nothing. Anything he said would have been the equivalent of throwing oil on a fire, he knew that.

'I thought you were trying to protect me... God, an old man who has never done anyone any harm and you set out to—'

'Enough, Anna. I understand you're upset, but this is no conspiracy. I'm sorry, but your grandfather is guilty of everything he is accused of and more. He has a dozen aliases. When he was in Iceland he used the identity of a dead boy. He was my father's partner. He embezzled from the firm and left my father to carry the can.'

'You're rich…you planted the evidence!' she yelled wildly.

He caught one of her flailing arms and lowered his voice to a soothing tone intended to reassure the dogs, who were looking unsettled by the commotion, as well as Anna. 'Calm down, you're going to hurt yourself.' He pursed his lip in a whistle and both animals settled down on their haunches.

Anna, who was pausing to gulp for air, didn't register the canine-human interchange as she pulled her hand free. She *had* been calm, she had been ice calm and then he had walked in and she had gone up in flames. She stood there shaking with the aftershocks of a mind-numbing rage she had never experienced the like of before.

She scanned his face.

'You're not even denying it?'

He found her subdued tone even more disturbing than her furious shrieking.

Anna swallowed a sob, hating that there was a tiny part of her that had wanted there to be an explanation, even though she knew in her heart that it wasn't possible.

'The truth is your grandfather is a crook. He

has ruined countless lives, including those of my parents. Perhaps the only good thing he has done in his life is take care of you.'

Her breath coming in short, sharp pants, Anna shook her head and covered her ears. 'You're trying to turn me against him. Well, it won't work,' she gritted. 'I *know* my grandfather.'

He picked up on the expression that flickered at the backs of her green eyes. 'But you're wondering, aren't you? That's why you're so angry. You have your doubts.'

Unable to quite meet his eyes, she looked past his shoulder. 'I have no doubts at all. Now, if you'll excuse me, I have some packing to do.'

'Come back, Anna. Go home, check out your grandfather, check out the facts and come back. We can talk...'

She looked at him as though he were insane. 'Talk...the only thing you ever wanted from me was sex and that particular well is dry!'

His jaw clenched. 'I don't seem to recall you complaining.'

'Oh, you were great. I can't wait to sell the story of my nights in the billionaire's bed to the tabloids, then I'll use the money to sue you,' she said, feeling quite pleased with her inspired fictional revenge.

'You wouldn't do that.'

'But you're not quite sure, are you?' she taunted.

'Anna.'

Not breaking her stride, she made her feelings clear with the use of a universally understood hand signal.

CHAPTER THIRTEEN

'I'M TOO LATE…?'

'I'm sorry.'

The matron curved an arm around Anna's shoulders and pulled her into the office, pushing the weeping young woman down into a chair.

'He slipped away quietly. There was no pain.'

'He was alone!' Anna sobbed, the tears spilling unchecked down her cheeks.

The older woman, her eyes soft with compassion, squeezed Anna's shoulder. 'I was holding his hand. He was not alone. No one here is ever alone. Would you like a few minutes to gather your thoughts?'

Mutely Anna nodded.

'I'll be back shortly with a nice cup of tea.'

'Do you know if anyone called my mother?'

'We tried to contact her when we were trying to call you, but there was no reply.'

Anna nodded and the door closed. She pulled out her phone, wiping her face on her sleeve, and dialled her mother's number. By some miracle it was picked up immediately.

'Mum, it's Anna.'

'Anna? Oh, Anna, darling, how lovely to hear from you. You naughty girl…you are such a stranger.'

'Mum, I have some bad news.' She took a deep breath. 'Are you alone?'

'No, Gregor is here and—'

Anna, eyes closed, teeth clenched, cut across her. 'Mum, Grandpa is dead. And I wasn't here.' Her voice shook and wavered. 'I was on a flight and I wasn't here!' she wailed.

'Anna, you know what crying does to your eyes. And not really a shock, darling—he wasn't young, was he?'

Anna gave a laugh of sheer disbelief and wiped the mist from her face again. 'And, Mum, I don't know whether you have read anything, but before he died there have been some horrible stories, the police are involved and—'

'Oh, he finally got caught, did he? I always told him he would be.'

The response took her breath away. 'Mum… you're saying it was true? You knew?'

'And you didn't? I assumed you would have realised by now—your grandfather, my dear, was a master con man. Your dad, of course, was very disapproving, but I always thought it was a bit of a hoot until the Iceland thing happened and that man killed himself. For a while Henry did behave himself, but old habits die hard and before long he was at his old games again. But, you have to admit, he was never mean to us, was he? I wonder what's in the will.'

Her mother's voice faded into the distance as her hand lowered and she cut her off.

She sat there, a blank look on her pale tear-stained face, staring ahead. Soren had been right about everything and he'd been searching for justice for his father... It all made perfect sense now. *He'd used her...* She had never been any more to him than a means to an end.

He had made her love him and he had never cared for her; she had been a useful idiot, that was all!

By the time the matron returned she was quietly composed, at least on the surface. Inside, her heart was a solid block of ice, it might never thaw, but she would never *ever* forgive Soren.

It was meant to rain at funerals but the day they laid her grandfather to rest the sun was shining. It felt wrong, but then a funeral could not feel anything but wrong.

'Right,' said Sara. She and Penny had been there to support Anna but, other than a couple of staff members from the Merlin Clinic and a couple who Anna suspected had come to the wrong funeral, but ended up staying to swell the sparse number, that was it.

Most of the charity trustees were either in jail or on bail or, in one case, in the middle of being extradited. And all of his friends had long vanished into the woodwork. Her mum, who it turned out had always known about her grandfather's nefarious activities, was spending the month in a retreat to equalise her out-of-balance chakras.

Penny and Sara had given her some time at the graveside alone before they decided to drag her away.

'So how about we have a little wake down the pub?' Penny said.

'I don't think—' Anna began.

'She'd love to,' Sara said over her head.

'I am here, you know.'

'*Here* being the most depressing place in the world, so let's go to the pub.'

Anna allowed herself to be dragged along, though she didn't drink the shots and her friends pretended not to notice.

'So who was the tall guy on the hill?' Sara asked during a lull in the rather forced conversation.

'What...?' She caught Sara's hand mid-shot. 'Focus, Sara. What guy on the hill?'

'The one who came late and didn't like to intrude. You know…your average six-four, godlike, stepped-off-Mount-Olympus figure in a really expensive suit.'

Anna's heart started to thud in her chest. 'Did he have blue eyes?'

'The man was like two hundred metres away. I didn't get the eye colour, just the general aura of yumminess.' She frowned a little blearily. 'Why? Is he someone I should know? Was it the guy off the telly who advertises…? What's-his-name…' She stopped, her eyes widening. 'You… A man… Wow, does that mean you finally—?'

'Hush, Sara, it's a funeral. Lower the volume.'

'A wake—the wakes in my family are seriously loud. If you don't get wasted, you're not invited again.'

Over her head Penny rolled her eyes. 'Well, I don't have your stamina so sorry, folks, I need my bed.'

'I'll walk with you,' Anna offered, and Penny mouthed her thanks over Sara's curly head.

It was slow progress, hampered by the fact that Sara had moved from loud drunk to sleepy drunk.

'She is such a lightweight,' Penny said affectionately as they both watched Sara's zigzag approach to the hotel steps. 'But you've got to love her, and she has been so worried about you.'

'I'm fine. Don't worry.' The two women embraced.

'Well, you know where I am if you need me,' Penny tossed over her shoulder as she hurried on her five-inch heels to catch up with her room-mate.

In no particular hurry to get back to her flat, Anna walked through the park.

She knew she ought to be feeling something, but she just felt empty and a little ashamed when she realised how desperate she had acted at the mention of a random tall guy.

She fished the key out of her bag and stood at the door of her flat. It was not a big space, but as all the stuff from her grandfather's house that hadn't already been sold—for which read worth-less tat—was stacked in cardboard boxes in her living room, the small space was even smaller.

As she put the key in the lock, a noise to her right made her spin round—a woman had been mugged two streets down only last week.

'I have a...' She paused, key in fist, and almost slid down the wall that her visitor had just slid up with a sinuous grace that made her stomach flip in a way she remembered very well.

'What are you doing here?' she asked, tipping her head back as he reached his full impressive height.

They were both dressed in funereal black but

there the similarity stopped. Despite the fact he had presumably been sitting on the floor, there was not a crease or a speck of dust on him.

Her suit was creased and some of the crisps that Sara had sprayed on her when she'd laughed had stuck to her jacket, she hadn't looked at her updo since eight a.m., so she was assuming it could use some work, and her lipstick was long gone.

He wasn't wearing lipstick...his mouth... She swallowed and suddenly wanted to throw herself at him.

She controlled the impulse.

'I said what are you doing here?'

Now she noticed he didn't look so hot—not creases, but there were very dark shadows under his eyes and he'd lost weight, which had sharpened his features. Haggard was going too far but he did not look the picture of health.

'What are you doing here?' she repeated again.

'I came for you.'

Her brain said caution, her heart said... She was not going to be misled by her heart any more.

'You'd better come in, but I'm warning you it's a mess.'

'Fine.' He stepped over a packing case before she thought to warn him about it.

Outside he looked bad, inside he looked awful,

in a gorgeous way, of course. 'You look terrible. When did you last sleep?'

'I came to apologise.'

'What for? You were right. My grandpa was an evil monster.' An evil monster that she had just put into the ground.

He watched her beautiful lips quiver and brutally quashed the urge to put his arms around her. It was a privilege he had lost, but one he had every intention of winning back. 'You got to see him before he...died?'

'I went straight to the clinic after I got off the flight,' she recalled. 'They'd been trying to contact me all day. He'd already slipped into a coma. Were you there...at the funeral?'

'You saw me?'

'No, my friend, Sara, she described you. So, Soren,' she said, feeling quite proud of how civilised she was being, 'what does bring you here?'

'I have already said. I came for you.'

She shook her head, unable to stop her traitorous heartbeat quickening. 'Me as in...?'

'Just you.'

'Are you mad?'

'If it will win me any brownie points, definitely, I'm certifiable. But if not, I'm not mad, just desperate and willing to... *Dio*, Anna, I am so, so sorry,' he groaned. 'What happened was all my fault. You were right in everything you said about me except one. I never wanted to hurt you. I only ever wanted to protect you.'

'But you were right. My grandpa was a crook. He was responsible for your father's death and others too,' she admitted heavily. 'I think I must have known at some level, I *should* have known, but he was always so good to me.'

'No one is all black. There are shades of grey.'

Not according to the police, who, once they had established to their satisfaction that she was not involved, had been willing to show her the proof of her grandfather's guilt.

His death had meant, they had explained, that she was not obliged to back any financial recompense to those he had cheated. Legally she could keep the house, which, it transpired, her grandfather had transferred to her name.

Anna hadn't wanted any of it. It was all sold, the proceeds going to his victims, except for the stuff in the boxes that no one wanted.

'I said some terrible things to you and I don't expect you to forgive me,' she said.

'There is nothing to forgive. I should not have let you find out that way—I was a coward,' he declared, drawing a startled look from Anna. 'I knew what you would think if I told you, and I could not bear the idea of you seeing I was no hero. The guilt every time you said thank you and—'

'Soren…you said you *came* for me. What did you mean?'

'Just that, I came for you, to take you back with me. I know I have a lot to prove, but you belong with me. It is true when I first met you I thought, I *wanted* you to be guilty too…but in my heart and my body I knew you were innocent. I just wouldn't let myself believe… I couldn't trust my instincts.

'I was a coward, Anna. I have been so stuck in the past, convinced that revenge would free me from the nightmares, but it didn't, Anna, my sweet, beautiful Anna, you did. I have been afraid of committing to a future… You are my future and I didn't recognise it until it was too late… It's not too late and I won't leave without you… You're crying?'

'Of course, I'm crying.' She sniffed. 'I've been so lonely, loving you, thinking you hated me, thinking of those terrible things I said to you… and you made me feel beautiful—'

'Enough!' He cut her off with an imperative slashing motion of his hand. 'You love me?'

She nodded.

His fierce grin flashed white and he grabbed her, hauling her into him. 'Then the rest it is—'

'Kiss me, Soren,' she said, her eyes on his face. 'Just, please, kiss me. I've been so lonely.'

'You will never be lonely again, *cara*,' he promised.

It was two weeks since his grandfather had told Soren he would disinherit him if he married her and two weeks since Soren had told him to go to hell.

Biagio had been bluffing and he had realised that Soren was not—he was now the guest of honour at their engagement party. In fact, his attitude had undergone a total change to the extent he had personally taken control of the guest list for tonight, which was why the intimate dinner was now a ball for five hundred.

Soren had wanted to confront him, but Anna had persuaded him to let his grandfather get on with it if it kept him happy.

She was trying to decide on her earrings—the diamond drops were nice, but Soren said the emeralds matched her eyes—when there was a tap on the door.

Anna adjusted her robe and yelled out, 'Come in.'

'It's only me, Anna.' Hanna Steinsson came in. 'I hope you don't mind. Soren said you wouldn't.'

'Of course not. What a pretty dress. You look lovely.' Her future mother-in-law was looking very youthful in a pale lavender crepe ankle-length bias-cut dress.

'Thank you. There are a lot of people here already.' Her eyes went to the red dress. 'You will look stunning. What a shame your mother can't be here.'

Anna smiled. In the short time she had known her she felt closer to Soren's mother than she did her own.

'I can't decide what earrings to wear—what do you think?'

'Well, actually, I was thinking, I was hoping… When Soren said you would be wearing red, and with your colouring…' She put a padded velvet box on the dressing table. 'Open it. I would like you to have them. They were my own mother-in-law's once.'

Anna opened her box and gasped. Inside lay a string of fire opals and a pair of chandelier earrings.

'They are beautiful and far too much. No…' She shook her head. 'I really couldn't take them.'

'It will make me happy if you do.'

Tears sprang to Anna's eyes. 'You are so kind. I was sure you'd hate me because of who I am.'

The older woman bent and kissed her cheek. 'Anna, my dear, you are the woman my son loves and that is who you will always be to me. I just wanted to say how happy I am for you both now, because I know you will not be offended if I slip away early… I struggle with the crowds, you know.'

Anna sprang to her feet and hugged her. 'I think I wouldn't mind coming with you.'

Hanna shook her head. 'No, my dear, you have a good time—this is your night and I know that Soren wants to show you off.'

When Soren came in a little while later the dress was still on the hanger but she had finished her make-up and was wearing the opals.

'Mum will be happy to see you wearing those.'

'She is lovely, Soren.'

'I knew it was a mistake to let him invite half the damned world tonight. Biagio is down there now inviting everyone to our wedding, telling them to keep Christmas week free.'

'Ignore him,' Anna soothed as she shook out the red dress and laid it on the bed. Without the confidence she had gained from being loved by Soren she would never have had the poise, the sheer nerve, to appear in public in something that was so…revealing, so in-your-face sexy.

'Are you going to be able to dance in those shoes?' he asked, looking at the spindly heels she had selected.

'I can always take them off.'

He grinned. 'So long as you put them back on when we're in bed.'

Anna struggled to pretend outrage.

'So how are thing going down there?' she asked warily. She had strayed into the organised chaos early when it became obvious that organised was debatable. She had not put up too much resistance when Soren had got all masterful and removed her from it.

He sat down on the bed. 'Do you really want to know…?'

'Ooh, that bad?' She shook her head. 'Definitely not. I shall just waft in there looking sexy and beautiful.'

'You always look sexy and beautiful.'

'You are a dutiful fiancé and I will reward you.'

'I am relying on it.'

'But tonight I'm making a big push-the-boat-out glam-up effort.'

'Fair enough, it will be much appreciated. One thing I should warn you about… Biagio has brought his…*friends*…'

Her face dropped. 'No, seriously…both of them?' His grandfather, who was suffering from what Soren called a displaced alpha male syndrome and Anna called a second childhood, had two twenty-somethings in residence with him on his yacht.

'It's window dressing. He's not actually *doing* anything with them—he's eighty, for God's sake!'

'They've not come in bikinis, have they?'

'They are wearing clothes...sort of.'

'I can't wait,' she responded, straight-faced.

'Let's face it, it's not as if anyone is going to be looking at them, is it? Not with my lovely fianceé there,' he purred, dragging her down onto his knee and sliding his hand inside her silk robe to massage her breast. He stopped when she winced. 'Is something wrong? Did I hurt you?'

'No...nothing is wrong, Soren,' she said, laying her hand against his cheek. 'I'm just a bit tender...'

Sudden comprehension lit his face, his expression changed and wonder slid into his eyes. 'That is why you didn't drink any champagne last week.'

She'd thought nobody had noticed she was drinking sparkling water. 'I wasn't sure then, but I am now... It's early days,' she warned. 'I don't want to go public yet...but I do think maybe we might not want to wait for a Christmas wedding. Maybe a nice small village wedding next month with our friends?'

Soren laid a protective hand on her flat belly and kissed her lips deeply.

'It will be our private secret for as long as you wish.'

'You do know that the plus side to this is I might actually get boobs? Mum will approve.'

At the mention of her mother his expression darkened. He made an effort for Anna's sake, but he would never be able to relax in the company of a woman who had not appreciated the gift she had been given. As always, he experienced a rage when he thought of her, made worse because he knew it was powerless, but he accepted it for Anna. The self-absorbed woman did not have the emotional intelligence to ever comprehend what she had done to her daughter.

'Don't worry, I won't be telling her, but your mum, if you don't mind...?' She was pleased to see the look of delight she had hoped for on Soren's face. She would have made a point of cultivating a relationship with Soren's mother in any case, but she took a lot of pleasure from the relationship.

'She will love being a grandmother.'

Anna swung her head, holding her rich hair back from her face to look at the man beside her. 'Scary or what?'

'I imagine all prospective parents feel that way—one perfect new life to mould. It is quite a responsibility. But you will be a perfect mother.'

Anna grinned, but tears prickled her eyes. So much could go wrong that she didn't want to take anything for granted, but she knew that a baby,

Soren's baby, would make her life too perfect to be true. 'The next eighteen years or so will tell.'

'And now,' Soren said, breaking the mood as he leapt to his feet and clapped his hands, 'it is my responsibility to get you into that dress and onto that staircase.'

'Couldn't I just slip in a side door?'

He produced one his best autocratic alpha looks. 'My wife-to-be, the mother of my child, does not slip in through side doors. I want the world to see what a lucky man I am.'

'Lucky, yes, you are, but world…quite a lot of people would be more accurate.'

He stood there looking at her. 'Are you ever going to get dressed? You are so last minute.'

'I have my face on, my hair is done, there is a reason for the fact my dress is on the bed and not on me,' she said, unfastening her gown to reveal the strapless bra and French knickers she wore underneath before reaching for the sliver of red silk. 'I get ready early and you undress me, which makes me late and flustered.'

His eyes darkened dangerously. 'Is that a challenge?'

She whisked away laughing and slipped into the bathroom, locking the door behind her just to be on the safe side—when it came to Soren a lock was a useful supplement to her non-existent willpower.

'Wait downstairs!'

Soren looked at the locked door, an expression of frustration on his face. 'Don't you trust me?' he complained.

The response did not try to spare him. 'No... I look very hot—you wouldn't be able to keep your hands off me.' She looked in the mirror as she spoke. She was only half joking; she barely recognised the person staring back at her. The dress was *just* right. It managed to make her look as if she had a bust, which was a minor miracle, and it made her long and...*sinuous and sexy.*

At the top of the staircase Anna paused and thought, head back, chest up, girl, and began her descent, hoping like hell she didn't fall off her heels.

It was the hush followed by murmurs and a collective gasp that made Soren turn his head. He was frowning, having just managed to fight off the clinging attentions of one of his grandfather's bikini bimbos.

Soren stilled, the tightness in his chest making it hard to breathe as he watched his lovely future wife float down the staircase. He roused himself from his stupor and walked out to greet her, bowing formally at the waist as he took her hand.

Their eyes connected.

'*Tesoro mio*, you do indeed look...*very hot.*'

He pulled her into him, moving from just friends to lovers with a smooth adjustment, then smiled and thought, *Better...much better.*

Together they circled the empty floor to the strains of the orchestra, but actually they didn't need the music. They were moving to a very different tune, a tune they both remembered well.

EPILOGUE

ANNA FROWNED. 'The priest is here. Everyone's in the chapel. They're waiting.'

Sara, who was admiring her godmother's hat in the mirror, turned around. 'Well, it's not like they can start without them, is it? No babies... no doting dad, no christening—not rocket science.'

'I know you're right, but I simply don't know where they can be.'

'Oh, I don't know. In one of the twenty million rooms in this place...? Me, I would happily live in any of your bathrooms. The interior designer had a serious fetish, not that I'm complaining. I get so turned on by plumbing.'

'I'll go check the... I'll go check.' She stopped. Sara wasn't listening to her; she was staring with a soppy smile at the ring on her left hand. Since her engagement to Franco she'd been doing that a lot.

Anna glanced in the mirror to check herself

out. The babies were only three months and most of her baby tummy was gone, mainly because she was never still. Twins did not allow for much down time. She didn't know how she would have coped during the early weeks when the babies wouldn't sleep and she was shattered without Soren, who had turned out to be a very hands-on dad.

When he'd announced he was taking paternity leave his grandfather had been outraged, but since the babies had arrived he had calmed down. His boast was that only a *real* man, a Vitale, could father two babies…even if one was a girl.

Evangeline had been born first, her bright blue eyes so like her father's wide open; Arturo had come a half-hour later. Smaller by a few ounces, he'd spent his first few nights in special care.

He had caught up now to his sister and had a fine pair of lungs, eyes as green as her own and, according to his father, a temper just like hers too. Anna still found herself waking him to check he was breathing.

He'd been breathing all right last night. She hadn't had a wink of sleep and, after they had both been dressed, Soren had offered to have them so that she could get ready in peace.

Now she was ready and the guests were all in the chapel but the babies and their father had vanished...where...? A slow smile spread over her face as she began to retrace her steps, suddenly sure where she would find them.

Her instincts proved dead on.

She walked into the ballroom, empty but for the candles burning in the windows and the solitary figure, a baby in each arm, who was circling the floor.

She walked across to join him.

'You vanished,' she whispered, looking down into the face of each sleeping baby. 'They are so cute when they are asleep. Why didn't you tell me where you were going?'

'I knew you'd figure it out, and you did.' His logic was inarguable.

'You're impossible,' she complained without any conviction.

He flashed his devil-on-steroids smile and her knees went weak. 'People are waiting.'

He shrugged. 'I wanted to show the babies where I fell in love with their mother.'

'Did you?'

'I think I fell in love with you the first time I saw you, but I was too scared to admit it even to myself, but that night, it was special.'

Throat thick with tears of emotion, Anna

nodded and slid her arms around him to complete the circle.

'I think our children are very musical.' He gazed down with paternal pride at the infants in his arms.

'Isn't it a bit early to tell?' she ventured with a smile.

'They recognised *our* song straight away. They obviously get it from me.'

Her lips quivered. Her husband had many talents, but musical…? 'You're tone deaf, Soren.'

'I don't hear the music with my ears,' he retorted. 'I hear it with my heart, where you are, *tesoro mia*.'

To hell with her make-up. Anna let her tears flow…tears of joy. 'Keep me there, Soren,' she whispered.

She knew he would.

* * * * *

Swept away by Innocent in the Sicilian's Palazzo? *Why not get lost in these other Kim Lawrence stories?*

A Passionate Night with the Greek
The Spaniard's Surprise Love-Child
Claiming His Unknown Son
Waking Up in His Royal Bed
The Italian's Bride on Paper

Available now!